Velvet Ropes:
The Ties That Bind Mothers And Daughters

Lynda Linke

ISBN 978-1-62141-215-1

Published in the United States by Booklocker.com, Inc.

Printed in the United States of America on acid-free paper.

Booklocker.com, Inc.
2012

Velvet Ropes:
The Ties That Bind Mothers And Daughters

Lynda Linke

For my Mom –
I can never thank you enough.

and....
For all the women who shared their stories with me.

Contents

Introduction

Being mothered by someone is a universal experience most of us share. Most of us were raised by our birth mother but many of us received mothering from other special women in our lives. Some of us were adopted, some of us had a foster mother with whom we'll always maintain ties, and some of us were raised by grandmothers, aunts, or in a multi-generational household where child rearing was shared. Grandmothers often play a big role in our lives, providing us with an unconditional love our mothers may not have been capable of giving. My mother has many fond memories of her maternal grandmother, who lived with the family for most of my mother's childhood and helped with child care and household chores while both her parents worked.

No matter whom it was that provided your primary mothering, she influenced your personality and left an imprint on your psyche that you will carry with you forever. For many of us the love and acceptance we were given helped us develop the confidence to become strong, well-adjusted women. For many others our relationship with our mother evoked feelings of inadequacy and a longing for love that lead us down paths of self-destructive behavior or into therapy to try to learn to love ourselves. Some of us wanted to be exactly the same kind of mother to our children as the mother we had; others tried to be as different as possible. We learned a lot about relationships with men by watching her. At some point in our adult lives, sometimes not until after we have children of our own, we usually come to understand that our mother did the best she could and we learn to forgive her faults and mistakes.

There are as many different types of mother-daughter relationships as there are mothers and daughters but there are certain commonalities they all share. As you read the stories in this book you will notice certain threads that run through all of them. Love is always one of the ingredients in the mix but not always in equal measure. Sometimes we love our mother but don't really like her as a person. Sometimes, due to misunderstanding and misplaced emotions we weren't able to have an adult relationship with our mother until much later in life. Sadly, some of the women in this book lost their mothers just as they themselves were entering adulthood.

A feeling of obligation toward our mother is sometimes stronger than an actual feeling of love and many of us just clench our teeth and fulfill our obligations as the "good daughters" we are expected to be. It is an interesting phenomenon that even a child who was abused or neglected will feel deep love and loyalty for her mother, although sometimes the only way for her to be a healthy adult is to find a way to leave that relationship behind. Fortunately, most of us haven't had to survive that kind of trauma.

I have collected stories of mother-daughter relationships, all written by the adult daughters, and included my own story. They are all true stories, although some of the names have been changed. I enjoyed reading these stories and I'm grateful to everyone for sharing them with me and allowing me to publish them. Some of them touched me deeply with their honesty. Many of them have lost their mothers and so, their stories have a special poignancy. I hope that when you read these stories you will find parts of yourself and your mother, or the woman who raised you, in all of them and feel a connection with all the women who have shared their stories with you. I'm sure their stories will evoke memories and I hope those memories make you smile.

Lynda Linke

Section I

Growing up without a mother….

Eva
Angela

What do girls do who haven't any mothers to help them through their troubles?

~Louisa May Alcott

My mother, Ella, was born on December 15, 1926 in Hyllinge, Sweden. She was the oldest of three girls. She didn't attend college and her jobs outside the home included work in a butcher shop and as a cook. She married my father when she was 24 and had the first of her two children, a boy and a girl, at the age of 26. My memories of my parent's relationship are good ones. I remember them as happy and caring with each other and, to this day, my father still says she was the only one for him.

My mother passed away when I was 10 and my life was never the same. Growing up without a mother was not easy. A father cannot be both. I was constantly seeking something; a mother, a security, a friend. Sometimes I didn't know what I was seeking. There were nights I cried myself to sleep because the hole in my heart could never be filled. Everywhere I went I was looking at girls, teenagers, women who had their mothers by their side. It was a constant aching and longing in my heart. I was even jealous sometimes. When my friends were nasty to their mothers I went home and cried because life was so unfair. I can remember thinking "here they are with a mother and they are so rude to them and I have nobody".

I do remember little things about my mother. She was fair and honest. She also could be tough sometimes, which made me a little afraid of her. She was very firm in her way towards my brother and me because she wanted us to grow up to be good honest people. We had hard rules to follow. I was only 3 when I started to make up my own bed, do the dishes, clean the table, etc. I raised my children in much the same way but not to the extent that they were afraid of me. I cook the way she taught me, which is always from scratch and with a lot of vegetables. I love to cook and plan parties and I always wanted to be like her when I was with her in the kitchen.

My mother was a little on the heavy side and I didn't want to be like that but I understand now that she was hypothyroid and was heavy because of that. Even though she was sick most of my life she was always active. She exercised constantly and made sure my brother and I did the same. She taught us to appreciate nature and respect it. We had to always go outside every day for hours, no matter the weather. She showed us the importance of fresh air to be able to function properly. That is probably the reason I became interested in natural health and the profession I have today. She used herbs from her garden when my brother and I were sick and we rarely visited a doctor. I learned from her that true beauty comes from the inside.

I believe that if she had been with me in my life we would have had confrontations. I am stubborn and so was she. She had a tendency to interfere in her sisters' lives because she thought they were not fair to their parents. My mother was very upset because she thought they misused their parent's trust. She just could not stand it when people were mistreated. Seeing all this helped to form my beliefs to never take advantage of other people, always show respect, be generous, but not let others take advantage of me either.

Eva
Certified Family Herbalist, Licensed Esthetician, wife, mother

My mother, Darci, was born in 1946 in Ontario, Canada and she died in 1980 in Virginia. I was only 8 when she died but I remember a lot of things about her. My sister, Sarah, was 13 and she helped me to keep Mom's memory alive, too.

Mom had two older sisters, Renee and Celia, who lived near us and they were all very close. Sarah's father died in Vietnam and my father disappeared after he and Mom got divorced when I was 3 so, Sarah and I went to live with our Aunt Renee, Uncle Don, and our cousins, Mark and Matthew. When I look back on it as an adult I realize that Aunt Renee and Uncle Don really had their hands full with us but they made us feel loved and welcome in their home right from the first day. Mark and Matt were teenagers, young men really, but they never made us feel like we were intruders. In fact, it was Matt, who was a Junior in high school and a star on the baseball team when we came to live with them, who gave me a love of baseball that I still have.

We were very lucky to have such a good family to take care of us but we always knew Renee and Don were not our parents. I don't mean that in a bad way. They wanted us to remember our mother. Aunt Renee always told us stories about our Mom and reminded us about how much she had loved us. She told us that Mom didn't have it easy but she worked hard to give us a good home. She told us about Mom's childhood and the fun the three sisters had together – and also the fights they used to have!

Mom got married and had Sarah when she was very young and then she ended up being a very young widow. She worked as what they used to call a "Gal Friday", which today would be an administrative assistant and she met my father when she was working for a company that manufactured airplane parts. Aunt Renee said she thought Mom was lonely and vulnerable when she met him and fell for his good looks and charm. Mom hadn't had much fun in her life and he took her dancing, to the movies and dinner. She was petite and pretty, with dark hair and eyes and I'm sure he must have been taken with her. I remember that she liked to sing and she smiled and laughed a lot. Aunt Renee said she had a good sense of humor and could do impersonations of movie stars and even people they knew. She used to make them laugh all the time and I can imagine that because both Aunt Renee and Aunt Celia are funny and have great attitudes about life.

I can't really talk about what kind of relationship I had with Mom because I was so young when she died. She was just my Mommy and she loved me and made me feel safe. I loved to be with her because she made everything fun, even housework. I don't know what it would have been like as I grew up but Sarah always said that Aunt Renee was more like Mom than Aunt Celia so I guess I can tell from the way I have gotten along with her what kind of relationship I might have had with Mom. When we went to live with Renee and Don we were both traumatized – in a heartbeat our lives were changed from one of security and stability to one where we had no parents and had to leave our home. I know I was a mess and I cried myself to sleep every night for a long time and had nightmares that woke me up. I remember Aunt Renee coming to my bed and rocking me in her arms until I stopped crying and then making me Ovaltine or hot milk with honey. During those nights I bonded with Aunt Renee in a way that Sarah didn't.

There were times when I was growing up that I missed not having my Mom and I know I took it out on Aunt Renee. As ggod as she was to me, I think I still felt angry and sorry for myself sometimes. Aunt Renee taught me how to sew, how to cook, how to fix things and, most of all, she taught me how to be strong and have respect for myself. She was very feminine but also knew how to stand up for herself. She also taught me how to laugh at myself. She was a teacher and her job was important to her so I grew up with a good example of a woman who combined a career and a family. Both she and Uncle Don encouraged us to get an education and learn to be independent. Looking back, I think part of that was because they wanted us to be able to take care of ourselves no matter what happened in life.

Renee and Don had a good marriage. They had a lot of fun together and I still have the image in my mind of them slow dancing on the deck long after a party was over. I don't remember ever hearing Uncle Don yell at anyone but sometimes Aunt Renee would lose her temper and anybody in her path better watch out because they would get a tongue-lashing! An important thing about marriage that I learned from them was to be able to admit when you're wrong and never hold a grudge. Uncle Don used to say "Do you want to be happy or do you want to be right?" Sometimes when one of us was really frustrated we'd yell back at him "I want to be right!" and he would crack up laughing and then, of course, we would, too. I know that Uncle Don's kind heart and easy going nature influenced the kind of men I was attracted to and eventually the one I married.

I have always missed my Mom in my heart but I know that I was blessed to have Aunt Renee to pinch hit for her. When I think of "Velvet Ropes" I think of soft ropes connecting me forever to my Mom through my Aunt Renee.

Angela
Teacher, wife, mother, niece

Section II

Losing a mother too soon....

Yvonne

Jonella

I am the woman who holds up the sky.
The rainbow runs through my eyes.
The sun makes a path through my womb.
My thoughts are in the shape of clouds.
But my thoughts are yet to come.

~Poem of the Ute Indians

My mother was born Ora Marie in 1909 in Key West, Florida. This made her a native "Conch". Her parents were also Conchs, having been born in the Bahamas. She seldom left the island and I'm not sure if that was because she didn't want to live anywhere else or because there was just no opportunity for her on the "mainland". She had six sisters and one brother...that's counting just those who survived infancy. Ora and one other sister remained in Key West for their entire lifetime. It's not easy for me to think about my mother without recalling memories of other important influences in my life like my father, brother, and my second cousin "Sue", who played more of the role of a grandmother.

You might think that Mom's family was a little strange but, if you got to know them, you would realize that they were just simple island people. None of them ever went by their real given name. Ora, or "George" as she was called by her siblings, was third oldest in birth order. She was the oldest who remained in Key West and I believe it was for that reason she became the "mother hen", the one who shouldered the worries and responsibilities for the others. The other siblings were: Ruby (Artie), Lulie (Tom), Ilma (Fung), Claudia (Phenie), Gladys (Jane) and Jack (Dick). Uncle Dick was the youngest and fought alcoholism his whole life. We kids loved him. He was clever, told jokes, did magic tricks and carved little toys out of wood. He lived with us for awhile when he was drying out one time but lost his job and moved back to Miami. Artie was the one who could do the table tipping or "talking to the Spirits" as it was called.

Mom married my Dad, Paul Joseph, when she was 26. Most women back then married much younger so I'm not sure if she was waiting for "Mr. Right" or if she remained single because of family responsibilities. She was very bright and talented but never had the opportunity to further her education or start a career. She went to work when I was about 6 years old out of necessity because Dad had a serious heart attack and was also afflicted with post polio disease. My brother and I were sheltered from the bad news at the time and were shuttled off to spend a summer with Dad's step sister and his step mother in Mineola, Texas while he was treated. He might have had surgery but no one ever shared the information with us. That summer Mom got a job as a bookkeeper with City Electric System where she worked the rest of her life. The people there were caring and family-like. She made many lifelong friends there.

Because of Mom's work schedule, we were supervised after school by a cousin, Lucille (Sue). Sue was my dad's age and had a rough life...married an alcoholic who I seldom saw sober. His name was Harry but his nick name around town was Parakeet because when he was drunk he would mumble and sound like a parakeet trying to talk. When I was a teen, my parents got me a Parakeet and I named him "Harry". Other baby sitters were teen aged identical twins named Ruth and Alma. We called them both "Honey" and they were the "Honey twins" to everyone around town. They were Sunday School (Methodist) teachers and Brownie Scout leaders. That's where we got our first religious education much to the chagrin of our staunch high church Episcopal grandmother. When my brother was about 6, he decided that he wanted to go to the church where he was baptized so I followed along to St. Paul's Episcopal. It was walking distance from our house in the Telegraph Lane alley so it was not a problem for our parents. We were both going to Roman Catholic elementary school so we got that exposure also. Most of the nuns were very nice and seemed very lovingly concerned that because my dad had been baptized Catholic and my mom was not and their marriage was a civil one, that Paul and I were in fact illegitimate. I had no idea what that meant until years later.

My parent's marriage was secure. Back then, everyone stayed married. They must have had differences but I seldom heard them argue. No one ever raised a voice or a hand in my parent's household...except for me...I cried and pitched tantrums until I got my way. It didn't always work but I had a pretty good batting average in the "wear your parents down" department. I would describe my parent's marriage as one of respect with an old fashioned attitude about displays of affection or emotion and I am the same way. A little teasing and humor is okay but I get along best with men who are soft spoken and polite.

I have one brother, Paul. He is 11 months older and he was the favorite. The first born is always the favorite, isn't he? He was the smart one...really genius, but always reserved and quiet, much like our father. Being the "baby" and a girl, I found ways to become the princess and was very spoiled. My Dad often referred to me jokingly and lovingly as "Queen of the Pisswinks". Both parents were very patient with us and, believe me, the two of us together could be a challenge. Like my Dad, my brother loved to tease but I always seemed to have a trick up my sleeve and got the last lick in.

Mom was outgoing but in a very quiet way. She was always there to help whenever a friend or relative needed anything. To my high school friends, she was known as "Momma Moore"...the one who piled everyone into the old Chevy and took them for ice cream after church every Sunday and the one who would join in at slumber parties and keep the jokes going. Her children came first in her life and she let the world know that. She once threatened a nun who had struck my brother for not reading loud enough in grade school. That's another story!

I think she taught me to be strong and to believe that being female doesn't necessarily mean being subservient or weak. She was physically beautiful but never flaunted it. She championed the underdog and could always find a way to help those less fortunate. She actually enjoyed helping others and she made it fun, or so it seemed to me. She never expected pay back or praise and Lord knows she often deserved it.

I never got to be a mother in the usual sense but I did have a career working with challenging children and teens and, on several occasions, provided a temporary home for a few. Eventually, I took on my husband's children from his previous marriage. The two girls were 13 and 14 at the time. Yet another story!

My adult relationship with my mother was not much different than it was when I was a child. She was always there for me. She died when I was in my early 20's, just as our relationship had started to become one of friendship. We had a cruise to the Bahamas' planned that never materialized but I'm sure we would have had a blast. I hope she would approve of the choices I have made in my life but I'm sure there would be a few things that she would scratch her head at.

Velvet is a very strong fabric yet soft and also royal. Mothers are that way, or at least they should be. We should all treat them like royalty for the love and support they give us. The strong tie is always there and transcends time and even death.

Yvonne
Retired Social Services professional, animal advocate, wife, step-mother and grandmother

My mother, Mary Adriane, was born in Kansas in 1920. She grew up in numerous cities in Illinois. She had five sisters and a brother and was in the middle of them all.

She was first married at the age of 23. She went to college practically all of her life and she was an elementary schoolteacher both before she was married and throughout her entire life.

My mother never figured out the marriage path. She married, had two sons, divorced, married again and had a daughter (me) and two more sons. She divorced my father when I was three and she was pregnant with her last son and married again when I was twelve. That was her last marriage...he was an alcoholic and was abusive both to her and to the three children still at home. I married just three months out of high school to a good man and we remained married for five years. After that I was single for twelve years and then I married my present husband. The influence my mother had in my first marriage was that of trying too hard. The influence she has had in my second marriage is her kindness, her devotion, her humor, and her tenacity.

Mom did have a favorite child, my next younger brother from me. He is brilliant and always was from the first memories I have of him. I always felt that, as a schoolteacher, she gravitated toward such a gifted child. Also, he was the oldest male in her second set of children and, as she got older, I think she found some protection and comfort from him. He always took on a tremendous amount of responsibility, even as a father and husband. I always said that Mom didn't quite know what to do with a girl. I spent as much time as I could away from the house at my grandparents' home in another town. While I knew Mom was proud of me, her only daughter, at the same time I felt like she resented me somehow and was even jealous of me sometimes. I always felt like I was having to hold myself up. She did the best she could…we were poor as dirt and we all had to do our part.

My mothers' personality was amazing. She had a heart as big as the ocean (something she told me the night I told her I was going to get married). She loved to laugh and sing and play the piano, accordion, and organ. She loved teaching and taught her own children as instinctually as if she never had the normal parental questions. Everyone loved her. Now for the other side…the side that could be at home. Whatever we could do as children we would do in order to never make her mad. In retrospect, I see a lonely, broke, frustrated, overweight, and sad woman. Her life was so hard. She never pitied herself or allowed others to pity her; however, she would always readily accept handouts and comfort when offered. She always had time to read to her children, volunteer, and support others in their times of need.

If I had to boil it all down to one thing I learned from my mother it would be perseverance. Through all of her times of life – good, bad, or indifferent – she could find her way back to a smile and a kind word for someone who needed it more. Her life is now like a beacon for me in my tough times. No matter what life hands me – ever – my life will never be as tough as hers and in my good times her smile warms me. I consistently thank her for my character and always try to make her proud. Two of the lessons I taught my children were 1) you're all you've got and 2) sometimes you learn from others what you don't want to do or be in life. Both of those lessons were ingrained in me as I watched and learned from my mother; however, there was also the amazing lesson of giving when you think you have nothing to give. I often wonder how she was able to pull that off with the life package she was given. She taught me to always make time for my children no matter what I was in the middle of…listen to them...play with them...nothing is too much trouble...and that hug of the moment is the most important thing in all of life.

I remember acknowledging that all I had to do to have a happy marriage was to not be the kind of wife my mother had been; however, at this writing I realize that I really never saw my mother "in" her marriages, but rather just know the stories. She was always off somewhere else or we had an event when she was married to the alcoholic and I was too young to remember any other. Besides, we three hated how he disrupted our happy life, raised strictly Methodist and in church every time the doors opened; this new life was quite a contrast. Anyway, I decided that I must be absolutely subservient to my husband. I remember feeling guilty once for cashing my paycheck and buying a 25 cent éclair with a girlfriend. Wow, I've come a long way, baby!

Unfortunately, my mother died when I was 24, after a seven year battle with cancer and, because of the dynamics of our relationship, I never got to be a friend with her. We loved each other desperately but never learned how to communicate. I always said that we needed to have that one big fight, meaning I didn't really want to fight with her but, rather, I just wished that we could have had truth between us without the baggage. Now I feel that I can communicate completely and openly with her with a "heart and soul understanding" that I could never have imagined before.

I have always been an independent cuss, even as a little girl. I was imaginative, creative, and talented. I needed support more than approval. I made and still make my choices in life based on the background and morals my mother handed me and the lessons of my mistakes. I have many clichés that came directly from Mom that taught me life "is what it is". As far as approval from her is concerned, I never felt that she knew who I was at the depth of me. Probably because I was only 24 when she went away, still vacillating, she could approve or not approve and I didn't count on that very much. In fact, at 57, I wonder sometimes if I am still trying to "find myself" so at this stage I wonder if I ever would have been able to let her in.

"Velvet Ropes: Ties That Bind Mothers and Daughters" is an interesting conglomerate of meanings. The velvet indicates a softness I never knew. We had our tie and our bond and I still miss her every day. I always help folks to know when they lose their mother that "No one ever loves you like your Mom".

Thank you for allowing me to write the things I have said for years about my Mom. She was a very special woman who had such a hard life. I have questions for her every day.

Jonella
Businesswoman, spiritual educator, wife, mother, grandmother

Section III

Learning from mother by trying to be different than her....

Sandra

Marie

Carol

Melissa

Lorraine

Brenda

Some are kissing mothers and some are scolding mothers, but it is love just the same and most mothers kiss and scold together.

~Pearl S. Buck

My mother, Louisa, was born in 1928 on a farm in Oklahoma. She was the oldest of five children, with two sisters and two brothers. Life was very hard for the family and it got even harder during the Great Depression. Like a lot of Midwesterners, my grandparents decided to try their luck in California so, in 1934, they packed up their old truck and headed west with my mother and her younger brother and sister. They settled in the San Diego area, near a cousin who had moved there years earlier.

Mom always loved music. My grandfather played the banjo and guitar and he taught them to my mother, who also had a sweet singing voice. Mom said their entertainment was for the whole family to sit on the front porch on a Saturday night and sing and play guitar and banjo. All the kids were musical and, eventually, my grandfather got a second hand piano and some of them learned to play. Mom also loved to listen to the radio – both the music and the stories.

My mother described herself as the "good daughter" who never disobeyed her parents or gave them a moment's worry. She was expected to help with household chores and the care of her younger siblings and then, when her mother died giving birth to her fifth child, it became her full responsibility. She was only 13 but she became like a mother to her younger brothers and sisters. Mom dropped out of school at 15 so she could take care of the household. After that she didn't have many opportunities to follow any dreams she might have had. When the baby was old enough to go to school Mom began working in a factory and that is where she met my father, Ray. They "kept company" for three years before marrying in 1950.

My brother, Ray Jr. was born in 1951, I was born in 1952, and my brother, Terry, was born in 1954 so my mother had three babies in diapers at the same time. My father was a weekend alcoholic – All week he worked long, hard hours as a factory foreman and on Friday and Saturday nights he got drunk and took out all his anger and disappointment on his family. Sometimes Ray Jr. caught a beating but he was a quiet, sensitive boy and, most of the time, all he wanted to do was please my father and he usually succeeded. I don't know if it was because I was a girl and always small for my age or if there was some other reason but, he rarely hit me. Terry was the most like my father both in looks and temperament and that probably worked against him but he also didn't show any fear, which made my father even angrier. Terry got some terrible beatings but he never cried out loud. I can remember being curled up in my bed under the blankets and praying for my mother to step in and help Terry but she never did. I know that sometimes my father would give her the back of his hand if she spoke up to him when he was drunk but I have never been able to forgive her for not protecting her children. My childhood was full of fear, tension, and insecurity and I blame her as much as my father for that.

On Sundays we always got dressed up in our best clothes and went to church and then my mother's father and most of her brothers and sisters came to our house for dinner. She spent practically the whole day in the kitchen and I and my two aunts were expected to help her. As I got older I came to dread weekends and I didn't know which was worse – Friday and Saturday nights or Sundays. Sundays were a different kind of torture, with everyone acting like a normal family and my father playing the role of benevolent patriarch. My mother seemed to be playing the role of June Cleaver, right down to the pearls. Looking back now, I think it was her way of surviving. She wanted her father and her siblings to think her family and her household were perfect but that must have been a terrible strain.

I left home the day after high school graduation and I didn't speak to my parents for almost 6 years, mainly because my father wouldn't let me come to the house and my mother accepted his command without argument. I got a job in the office of a car dealership in a nearby town and shared a small apartment with a friend. I talked to Terry on the phone and once in awhile I arranged to secretly meet him but my father had told him that he was forbidden to speak to me. Ray Jr. had already joined the Army and was serving in Vietnam, where he died. When Terry was 17 he and my father got into a big fight and Terry finally hit back and my father threw him out. He slept on my couch while he finished his last semester of high school and then he joined the Army.

Six years after I left home my father had a heart attack and died and I finally spoke to my mother after his funeral. I still had a lot of anger toward her but I also was older and had more understanding for her situation. I think that for an uneducated, unskilled woman in the 1950's there were very few alternatives available and it would have taken a much stronger woman than my mother to leave a bad marriage and strike out on her own. I still don't understand how she could have stood by while my father beat Terry, and sometimes Ray Jr., the way she did. I have two daughters and I know I would lay down my life for them.

I don't know if my mother had dreams when she was young and I don't know what kind of a person she really was because I don't think I ever had an honest conversation with her. She was completely overshadowed and dominated by my father and she only lived three years after he died. Sadly, the most important thing I learned from her was that I didn't want to be anything like her as a woman, wife or mother.

To me "velvet ropes" are something that can slowly wrap around and choke you to death if you don't get away in time.

Sandra
Businesswoman, wife, mother, grandmother

My mother was born in Chicago in 1925. She was the only child of college educated parents, which was unusual for the time, especially for her mother to have gone to college. My mother was the third generation of only female children and I became the fourth. My grandfather was in the hotel business but the stock market crash saw the demise of the hotel industry so he packed up the family and they moved to New York City sometime around 1932. The family built a home in a new planned community in New Jersey. My grandfather went to work as the manager of a large paper producing company that was located just outside of New York City in New Jersey. My grandmother stayed at home and took care of the household duties.

As my mother told it, she was very popular in school and had many friends that she kept in touch with for years to come. She was elected homecoming queen and served on many school committees over her high school career. Upon graduation from high school my mother enrolled in college in Pennsylvania.

My father was wounded in WWII and met my mother at a party in New York City in 1945. After a whirlwind courtship they married in August, 1946, when my mother was 21 and they settled in PA so that they could both finish college. I was born while they were living in GI housing until my father graduated.

After my father graduated with a degree in business our family moved to upstate NY and my father went to work for his father, who owned a successful supply business. My mother stayed at home to take care of me but she also had a busy social life because my father's business required membership at various social and civic organizations. My mother busied herself with activities like bridge and garden clubs. My mother did not like to cook or clean and as a result I don't like those activities either. I had a very happy childhood and we lived in a neighborhood where there were many children to play with. Although my mother socialized a great deal, she also included me in many activities.

When I was 10 years old my grandfather decided to sell his business and take early retirement in Florida. My father was devastated that he would sell the business out from under his only son rather than pass it down. The result was that my father took a job with a competing company and they transferred him to another city in NY, about 60 miles east of where we lived. Looking back on these events it is clear that my mother was very supportive of my father but it must have been a difficult time in their lives. I don't recall ever feeling fearful or nervous because my mother treated the move like a new adventure.

We settled into our new home and my mother went about finding new friends and social activities very quickly. My father, on the other hand, did not fare as well and over the next few years it became apparent that he had a serious alcohol problem. By the time I was 14 or 15 years old he had lost his job, had gone to rehab a couple of times, and my mother had to find a job to support the family. She found a job as the executive director of a newly founded inner city community action agency. Her agency was one of many created in the mid 1960's as the result of civil rights legislation and the need to start grass roots anti-poverty programs.

My mother flourished in this new job. Her agency was a model for other settlement houses across the state. My mother became a successful fund raiser. She also developed excellent political skills; always knowing who she needed to talk to and getting the inside track on new funding sources or programs. My mother became a well known community leader and was invited to speak at many national conferences to describe the programs she had introduced and to share the data on the successes that her agency had produced. As I reflect on my mother's legacy I realize she was certainly a role model for strong women in business and she was ahead of her time in that regard.

While my mother was busy with her career I completed school at a Catholic girl's high school and my father eventually quit drinking and became a staunch AA member. One recollection of my high school years is my mother constantly insisting that I participate in as many activities at school as possible because colleges looked at well-rounded prospective students. This was certainly the theme of my mother's entire life – get involved and you'll get ahead. I was often embarrassed by my mother's assertiveness. She was very out-spoken and would give her opinion even if I thought she should keep it to herself. As a result of my feelings I did not like to have friends visit my house during my adolescent years. I much preferred hanging out at my friend's homes where their mothers rarely said a word. I did not have much interaction with my mother during these years since she was so busy working and trying to make sure my father was all right.

During this time in my life, I saw my mother change from a stay at home housewife to a strong business woman who was willing to stand by my father through all of his problems until, eventually, they reversed roles. My mother was the bread winner who supported and allowed my father to do what he felt was important for his recovery.

My father had his first heart attack at age 39 and he survived 8 more attacks before finally succumbing at age 53, leaving my mother a very young widow of 52. My father's war injuries and hard living definitely took their toll. My father did live to see his grandson who was 10 months old at the time of his death. Being a grandfather was a highlight of his life. My mother, on the other hand, was pleased to have a grandchild but was not a "motherly" type and did not like to care for babies. She did much better with my son once he was able to go to the movies and out to dinner with her, which was more to her liking. After my father's death, my mother continued to excel in her career and found some other widows to travel with. She was an avid antique collector and zealous shopper.

Our family consisted of just the four of us, my mother, husband, son and me. My husband was an only child also and his parents moved to Florida soon after we were married. We celebrated holidays, birthdays and got together regularly for several years following my father's death. Generally, my mother and I had a "girlfriend" type of relationship for a number of years.

My mother developed asthma as an adult and when she was diagnosed the dangerous side effects of Prednisone were not known. She took large doses of the drug daily for at least 20 years before problems started to occur. Over the years she ended up having 3 hip replacements due to bone deterioration and she was hospitalized with breathing problems a number of times. A definite role change occurred when my mother was ill because I had to be the caretaker but usually she bounced back from her illnesses and returned to her high powered job and life and things would go back to normal. All of that changed when she was 63 and she had a very bad asthma attack and had to be placed on a ventilator. Her ventilator was attached through a throat tube so she could not talk but she wrote notes and we developed a lip reading system as well. I visited my mother almost every day that she was in the hospital until the day she died, a Sunday when I chose to take my son shopping. I will regret that for the rest of my life. A senior center in the town in which we lived in NY is now named after her.

When I reflect on my mother's very strong-willed, controlling personality and her refusal to take no as an answer to anything, I know that I unconsciously saw her as over-aggressive and I have purposely taken a far more moderate approach to life. She was ahead of her time as a female business/community leader and she needed to be forceful to get ahead in a male dominated world but I did not like that behavior. I did, however, value my mother's approval in whatever I did. The fact that she was not thrilled with my choice of a husband was difficult for me to accept. My mother and I had a friendly adult relationship until she became ill and I had to take the caregiver role. At that point she struggled with her inability to take charge of everything but she had no choice. My mother and I loved each other very much but rarely spoke the words.

Marie
Administrative assistant, wife, mother

My mother, Angelina, was born on November 16, 1907. She and her twin sister were the second oldest of seven children born to Italian immigrants in what was known as the "Hell's Kitchen" Lower East Side area of New York City, where many poor immigrant families first settled. Her parents met on the boat when they were coming from Italy to the US with other family members. They married when my grandmother was only 16 and my grandfather, already established in his profession as a tailor, was in his early 20's.

As the family grew to three girls and four boys, of whom there were two sets of fraternal twins, they moved from Manhattan to the then open-meadowed suburb of Queens. They purchased a large two story home where the children grew to adulthood and in which my grandmother lived until her death. My grandparents were able to create their own little piece of heaven in their backyard with flower gardens and a vineyard reminiscent of their memories of Naples.

My mother enjoyed telling me stories about her early years, for example, how they would bring out the washtub on Saturday nights for their weekly bath, stoke the coal burning stove on cold mornings before going to school, lock their father in the basement when he would get drunk on his home made wine, and that her parents wouldn't let the children speak anything but English in the house so they would become full-fledged Americans. My mother was proud that she finished elementary school when so many of her peers were forced to leave school early to go to work. She always had great pride in being able to read and write.

She took on the role of "little mother" and helped her mother to take care of all her younger siblings. She was always very close to her mother and she expected me to take care of her when she was sick and in her older years, just as she had taken care of her mother. My mother and grandmother really took care of each other and understood each other; my mother being unofficially separated from my father and suffering from bouts of depression and my grandmother being a widow who also had a long history of periodic depression.

Mom walked more than ten miles each day to take the elevated subway train to work in downtown Manhattan before a trolley line was established. It was during a ride on that trolley with her twin sister that she met a dashing young man named Adam - my father. Judging by photographs taken to enter a beauty contest when she was 18 and, also on her wedding day, she was a strikingly beautiful girl and my father was taken with her. They began a five year romance and, finally, when she was 22, they were married. They had two daughters, first my sister and then, 18 months later, me.

Unfortunately, the marriage was doomed to be unhappy due to issues related to divergent cultures and their sexual intimacy and, after 16 years of marriage, they led separate lives. I was 14 when my father left the household and my memories are those of a child's feelings of fright, abandonment, desertion, sadness, anger, and confusion. My parents never talked to us about their break up but "things" were picked up through innuendo or from overhearing arguments while we pretended to be asleep. I didn't find out until I was in my 40's that many of the conclusions I came to about my parents' relationship were erroneous.

My relationship with my mother was a stormy one, mostly because of my own misunderstanding of the circumstances of her life. Fortunately, we were able to come together when I was in my 40's and had a new understanding of her and we had a peaceful, loving, adult mother-daughter relationship until her death. I know I have been blessed to have lived long enough to be able to gain some wisdom about the dramatic changes in my relationship with my mother that occurred over the years. I have come to realize the nature of my true relationship with my Mom and I have feelings of deep love, respect, and appreciation for who she was. I am so much more like her than I ever thought possible, in spite of working so hard to reject her and her ways during my teens, 20's and 30's. I was a rebel, running away from home at 17, rejecting the "wisdom" of my mother and blaming her for my father leaving us.

I know my "childhood perceptions" of my parents' marriage and the role each of them played had a profound influence on my relationships with men. It took me two failed marriages, counseling, a 12 step recovery program, and much self-help reading to finally discover, in my late 50's/early 60's, the nature of those influences and to successfully work on myself to reshape what I wanted in a marriage. I realized that I had selected men with similar character traits and attitudes as my idealized image of my father – dashing, fun-loving, romantic and also heavy drinkers. I subconsciously thought I was going to resolve my parents' unhappy marriage by being the "perfect partner", which I felt my mother hadn't been and which I childishly believed was the reason my father left. My mother was not trusting of men and, because of that; I was determined to be trusting to a fault, which led me heavily into denial of unacceptable behaviors.

My mother's personality was masked for most of my life by her schizophrenia (or so she was diagnosed when I was 19). Only from her 60's until her death at 83 did I see the "real" Angelina and come to know her as only an adult child is privileged to know their parent. She wanted to laugh and smile and be happy. She loved to go out to Italian and Chinese restaurants for dinner. When we were growing up she enjoyed taking us to every museum in NYC and to the beaches of Coney Island and Brighton almost every day during summer vacations. She was a New Yorker through and through, thinking there was no other place as sophisticated and wondrous as the "Big

Apple". She never traveled outside the United States and repeatedly stated that there was no place better than the U.S.A.

In Angelina's senior years I moved her to my home in Cleveland and then to a Catholic retirement home close to me. It was during this eighteen year period that I came to a new, more accurate, understanding of my mother. We grew quite close and made up for the many years of distance, (as much as this is possible). Many times I have thanked God for bringing us together so that I could honor her and take care of her in her older years.

The words/thoughts that come to my mind when reading the phrase "velvet ropes: ties that bind mothers and daughters" are: soft, slippery, rich and strong.

Carol
Retired Social Worker

My Mom was born in Massachusetts on August 7, 1968, where she also grew up. She attended a Catholic high school for 3 yrs and graduated from a public high school. Mom was the baby of the family. She has two brothers and a sister. She liked hanging out with the guys, mostly because the girls picked on her because she was not popular or thin like them.

I think she was married at 19 and had me. She did not go to college before I was born. I guess that is just how things work sometimes but I still think she is a pretty smart lady. We moved to Florida when I was almost three and shortly after we moved my Mom and Dad divorced. I don't remember a lot about how they got along because I was too young. The only thing I remember is my Dad got custody somehow and I was with him and my Grandma a lot. Not long after he married my first step mom, who I did not take to at all, and she is the one who raised me until I was fifteen. She and my Dad would not let me see my Mom very much even though the court said I was supposed to. If I was in trouble they often used as my punishment that I could not go see Mom.

I was my Mom's only child but I have two half brothers from my Dad. I really don't know why Dad got custody of me over Mom. He always told me bad stories about her but I don't have memories of any of the bad stuff Dad told me. Growing up with my Dad did have an influence on my relationship with men because I didn't like my Dad's attitude. He was a good father growing up but now I can't even stand to be near him and I made up my mind at a young age I would never be with a man who could do what he did to my Mom and just his personality in general. I still hold that promise to myself to this day. My husband is the best person in the world and I learned to judge men and people by being around the total opposite of my family. It may sound bad but sometimes that is what you have to do. I always dreamed of having a perfect family where everyone was close and loved each other and was always there. I guess you don't always get what you want.

My Mom has a good personality. She tries to be very outgoing, which is something I did not get a whole lot of growing up. I was very quiet because of always being put down by my step mom. I think if I would have grown up with Mom I would have been more outgoing in school. Since I did not see Mom very often I did not learn about what it means to be a woman but the little time we were together she was a good role model. When I turned fifteen I moved in with Mom and finally got to get to know her more. I knew her but we never got to have the bonding like most girls and their mothers so, as a teen just being with my Mom, I kind of reverted back to being Mommy's little girl. I would have her do my hair and rub my back every night. It sounds kind of silly but I just wanted what I never got to have as a child. At that time in Mom's life she and my step dad owned a restaurant and taught me how to run a business and how to deal with money and customers, even though sometimes you wanted to strangle them. Mom helped me to be a better student in high school. I had more freedom to be a kid instead of raising my two brothers like I had been doing, but I also had rules to follow and, boy, if I was two minutes late I was in trouble.

I learned how to be a good mother by doing the opposite of everything I saw growing up. My step mother was abusive both verbally and physically. Not having a close relationship with my Mom I did not get to learn from her so I had to learn by myself and I didn't want to be like anyone who raised me. I wanted better for my children and promised myself to not be anything like my family.

I became a mother early in life. Not the best thing to do and definitely not done on purpose, but that is what the good Lord had planned for me and I would not change that for anything in the world. That was a time in my life my Mom did not have a great influence on me because we had a big falling out and did not speak again for a while but we made up before my son was born and it all worked out.

As I said earlier, I made up my own mind about the rest of my life but every now and then I ask Mom for advice. I am not much of a talker about my problems because growing up I had no one to talk to and no one believed me about the problems at home. I was so confused about why I was not with Mom and I just didn't know what to think about the things Dad told me about her. I still often wonder why she didn't fight sooner for me and maybe she did but Dad kept us moving so much she couldn't always find me. When she did he would change our phone number or move. I am always trying to be different than Mom, such as being a better Mom and fighting for my kids, which I have had to do when their Dad moved to out of state but he didn't have a chance because I have more knowledge of family law than him. I always tell my boys I love them. They probably get tired of hearing it. Mom and I have become closer over the years but we missed out on so many things and so much time together that we don't have the bond I wish we had. I don't really understand the phrase "Velvet Ropes" because I don't have the tie that most women have with their mothers. Mom calls more now but I just don't know why I still don't hear I love you very much. I'm not sure why, but I do love her and cherish her and when I'm sick I still call her and cry to her even now as a grown woman.

Melissa
Nursing student, wife, mother

My Mom, Wanda, was born in St. Augustine, Florida, on October 30, 1925. My grandfather was a well driller and traveled a lot. My grandmother was an R.N. My Mom was the eldest of three daughters...and her father's favorite.

Growing up during the Great Depression made quite an impact on my Mom. Something else that influenced my Mom was losing her father to cancer when she was only about 16. This forced her mother to uproot the family and move to South Carolina so she could live with relatives and start working in a factory during World War II. After the war, my grandmother became an R.N., and so did my mother's sister. My Mom graduated from high school in South Carolina but, as soon as she could, she enrolled in secretarial school where she excelled. Later in life she would become a certified medical transcriber and work overseas in Saudi Arabia. More about that later.

My Mom moved to New York and became a fashion model. This is where she met my Dad. He was a good dancer and............well, here we are.....Mom had a way of encouraging people to reach their fullest potential. My Dad was moving appliances when he met my Mom. She encouraged him to use his financial wisdom, get a business suit, and apply for a job as a mortgage banker. With her prodding he got the job.

My Mom was elated at having two children. Like ME, she liked control. She sort of "ordered" one boy and one girl - and that's what she got. They had two children – first my brother, and then, three years later, me. In 1953 there was a polio epidemic in New York, and at 5 weeks of age I contracted poliomyelitis and was paralyzed from the neck down. My family couldn't afford expensive care for me..... But God had a plan. Remember my aunt was also an R.N., as my grandmother had been? She heard about Sister Kinney exercises for polio patients. My aunt taught these exercises to my Mom....50 exercises to be given three times a day. Without my Mom's perseverance, I would not be able to walk or maybe even be here today.

The doctors had advised my Mom to institutionalize me. Doctors said I'd never walk and *never* have a child. I'm glad Mom ignored their advice and diligently gave me the exercises I needed. Mom told me those exercises hurt me and I cried....and she cried. I can't imagine a love that could do that other than our Heavenly Father's love...doing whatever it takes, no matter how it hurts!!!! Needless to say, Mom proved the doctors wrong. I do have a wonderful daughter - and was able to pursue God's plan for my life in a major way because of the mother to whom He entrusted my care.

My parents divorced when I was in my teens, and I left home and lost touch with my Mom except occasionally. My mom was very hurt after the divorce and she moved to South Florida looking for a new start, prosperity, and the "good life". She loved to dance, go on cruises, and go to the beach. She worked as a medical transcriber at night so she could go to the beach during the day! She even got a great job overseas as a medical transcriber in Saudi Arabia. She called herself a "sun" worshipper and later, in November, 1984, she became a "Son" worshipper when she accepted Christ.

While Mom worked in Saudi Arabia, she sent home financial support to me when I took my daughter and left my first marriage. She tried to be supportive of me, and I knew she loved me.

After my father died in l984 she moved here to be closer to my daughter and me. We even tried living together in the 1980s - often unsuccessfully. We were both feisty and strong-willed. My daughter and my Mom always had a special connection. Mom would love to go to garage sales with my daughter until both of them were worn out.

For many years my Mom and I seemed to be on different "planets". I had become a Christian in 1982 and, although I was changing, I still had "baggage". My baggage at times clashed with hers and BOOM!!! (we could start our own luggage outlet!!); however, on November 25, 1984 my Mom came to Christ. I hadn't remembered the exact year but then two days before she passed I found her Bible in the nightstand at the assisted living. There, in her own hand writing, I read "Came to Christ November 25, 1984". I have the assurance and the hope that I'll see her again.

She was someone who enjoyed adventures; sort of a gypsy. My husband and I moved Mom an average of once per year from the time we got married in 1991. Before she was diagnosed with Alzheimer's disease around 2001 or 2002, I had already begun to help her keep up with her money. She tried for as long as she could to live independently and she also tried to live with us several times. WOE! That was a combustible situation. She and I clashed often in our earlier years. Mom was simply an independent woman who loved to live life to the fullest, and loved her family in her own quiet way. Mom leaves a legacy of strength and determination that lives on in me and my daughter.

God began working in our relationship...slightly. Forgiving each other and treating each other as the new creations we were was hard at times. John 4:44 says a prophet is not without honor except in his own country: sometimes family is the toughest to accept you as being changed, and vice versa.

As the Alzheimer's began to progress in my Mom's life, I saw changes, personality differences, and began taking more of a role in decision making. God gave me a dream in either 2004 or 2005 about seeing my Mom peeking around the corner of buildings in downtown St. Augustine. When I would run and look for her she'd be gone. Then, I would see her peek out from another building on another street. Running to where I thought she was, I'd find her gone again. A friend interpreted the dream for me, which turned out to be accurate. God was showing me that there were going to be times I'd see or recognize "the old mom" I knew. Then, she'd be gone. Then, another day or hour or week, I'd glimpse her again...and again she'd vanish. This happened over the next 5 or so years just as the dream symbolized. (Job 33:14-18)

I am grateful to the Lord for allowing my Mom to move to a closer assisted living facility. She loved some of the staff deeply –one in particular was like her "2nd daughter". We had a real party for my mom's 83rd birthday. We had a DJ who came to the assisted living facility and sang the songs of Frank Sinatra, Elvis, and the Big Band era. My Mom could hardly walk, but she was tapping her toe and trying to sing. She really enjoyed her day.

The owner of the assisted living facility was a blessing, too; she was very supportive and comforting to me. When I would call, she reassured me that Mom was okay and sometimes I would try talking to Mom on the phone. As the disease progressed, this became more difficult. When Mom wasn't having a good day, they would call me and I would "talk" to her and try to brighten her up. I am grateful for the gift that God and Hospice gave to us the last week of her life. I was able to spend some time with her every day...to talk to her...even get a smile from her sometimes. I was able to hold her hand...once I got brazen enough to rub her feet! Our family is not so "touchy feely" and I respected that about my Mom. In our family, we did not show affection a lot...we feed people! As my Mom got older, she was more open to hugs. I'm still learning myself.

I'm grateful to Hospice, who made sure Mom was comfortable. Having 24 hour bedside sitters assured me that my Mom was never alone. A scripture verse my Mom had written in her Bible was Isa. 43:18 "When you pass thru the waters..."

My Mom passed through many trials and sorrows. Much of this helped me to understand her and made it easier to forgive some things and accept her as she was.

My grandmother had been severely abused as a child, and so it affected how she raised her three daughters. My Mom was the oldest of 3 girls, and she was the scapegoat during my grandma's rages. My Mom had many emotional scars…some things I hadn't known about until after her passing.

For example, when my brother returned from Vietnam he was never the same. He was a transient, and disappeared finally in 1979 never to be seen or heard from again. I found a Christmas card from him sent from Vietnam in my mother's paperwork file that I didn't know she had. It was dated Christmas 1968. She never told me she had this card. It is very eye opening and heart wrenching.

I'd like to share these thoughts: 1. Forgive quickly….. 2. Love genuinely and don't assume you will have tomorrow - tomorrow may not come. 3. Let your "last journey" wishes be known to your loved ones ahead of time. 4. Grieve honestly; don't "stuff" emotions because you don't want to appear to be a Christian who lacks faith and trust in God (Remember Jesus wept over Lazarus - and He KNEW He was going to raise him again).

Lorraine
Founder and Executive Director of a non-profit agency, wife, mother

My mother was named Muriel and she was born in 1906 in Yorkshire, England. She was the youngest in the family, with two older brothers and two older sisters. I had the impression that she was her father's favorite and she might have been a bit spoiled by him or made to think she was special in some way.

My mother and father met when they were 18 and were married at 19. At the time of their marriage my mother was a laundress. Years later my older sister and I figured out that our mother had been pregnant with her when they got married. They had 6 more children; 4 girls and 2 boys. When I was a young child, around the age of 4, my mother's father died and her mother, my Grannie, came to live with us. Over the years, as more children were added to the family, Grannie helped a lot with child care and housework. I loved her and always felt much closer to her than I did to my mother. She was the one I went to with my problems or if I got hurt.

When I look back I know I didn't have a "bad childhood". We always had good food to eat, a nice home, clothes and shoes, and medical care when we needed it. We were kept clean and we were not abused. We were sent to school. I was a tomboy and I have many fond memories of playing outside with the boys from early morning until supper time. I grew up in England during the Great Depression and World War II and I know those were difficult times for many people and, looking back, I realize they were hard for my parents, too. My mother had to go back to work as a laundress, at least part time, to help support the family. My father was never unemployed as so many other men were but, I'm sure my mother's life didn't turn out the way she had hoped. We were poor but I didn't feel deprived and there were lots of other families that were in worse shape than us.

I don't know what my mother's dreams for herself might have been when she was a young woman but I suspect that she might have thought my father was a "catch" because he was from a better off family. She probably set her cap for him and thought she would have a nice life but, she was in for a surprise when his family disowned him after he married her. She actually had a nervous breakdown after her first child was born. My grandfather would not allow my father in the house but he would still visit his mother with one or two of us when his father wasn't home. I have memories of visiting my grandmother but none of my grandfather so I don't think I ever met him. My father had two older sisters and one of them was also disowned because her father didn't approve of the man she married but I do remember visiting my father's other sister. She had a beautiful home and only one child, my cousin Margaret. Margaret didn't have anyone to hand her clothes down to so my Aunt Elsie gave them to my father and I got lots of lovely things that were like new because we were the same size.

My mother was an uneducated woman who was ignorant in many ways. She didn't like anyone to read, even my father, so there were no books or even newspapers in the house. To this day, I still don't understand why she was like that but she wasn't the type of person you could question. She was narrow-minded and wasn't interested in discussion. She had many superstitions and I also think she had a sixth sense and could be quite intuitive at times. She never hit any of us but she did have a quick temper and a sharp tongue and she shouted a lot. She was always insensitive about the things she said, especially if she was angry or being spiteful. I think she was very high strung and probably had more than she could handle with seven children and not enough money for the kind of life she wanted. When she was younger she had dark hair and eyes and a nice figure. She had a nice singing voice and enjoyed the sing-along at the pub. I remember how pretty she looked in the high heels and lipstick she wore when she dragged my father to the pub on a Friday night. He was a quiet man and probably would have preferred to stay home and read or listen to the radio but he usually did what she wanted to avoid a fight. When she got angry she was like a hellcat and thought nothing of throwing things when she was in a temper.

I could never talk to my mother about anything and I learned at an early age that I couldn't tell her a secret. She is probably the main reason I have trouble trusting other women. She didn't know the meaning of privacy and had no qualms about going through drawers or opening mail. She was very nosey and she liked gossip but she didn't have any friends. She must have been an insecure woman because she had a lot of jealousy and envy toward other people, even her own children when they became adults. We weren't able to have relationships with each other or get together without her because she would always assume we had been talking about her behind her back and then would set about turning us against each other. She would twist your words when she told a sister or brother something you had said and the next thing you knew someone wasn't speaking to you. She used to upset me so much that sometimes I would get off the phone with her and cry. When I was almost 40 my husband said I was a grown woman with a child of my own and it was time for me to stop letting her control me. He was absolutely right and, from that day on, I didn't let the things she did and said bother me anymore. It's a shame that I had six brothers and sisters but I couldn't be friends with any of them and always had to be on guard about what I said to them. I blame my mother for that.

I think that subconsciously I wanted to marry someone who had the quiet qualities of my father but with a stronger character and I was very lucky to meet my husband when I was only 18. I knew right away that he was the one for me and we had a wonderful marriage and friendship for 59 years. I definitely didn't want the kind of marriage I grew up with. I wanted harmony and security and my husband gave me that. He also had a very good sense of humor and he made me laugh every day of our life together.

I also knew that I wanted to be a different kind of mother than the one I had. For one thing, I wanted my children to be able to come to me with their problems and secrets. I wanted them to feel that their privacy and their possessions were respected. As it turned out I only had one daughter but, we have had always had a good relationship and were able to enjoy each other's company as friends after she grew up. I had a lot of fun with her when she was a child and I enjoyed playing with her and teaching her to read and draw; things my mother never had time for or interest in.

Brenda
Wife, mother, grandmother

Section IV

My Mom is my best friend….

Tami

Heather

A mother is not a person to lean on but a person to make leaning unnecessary.

~Dorothy Canfield Fisher

When I was asked to come up with a story about my relationship with my mother, Bonnie, I was so happy to do it because I am the luckiest woman in the world to have the mother that I do. She is always there for me, my siblings, our children, and her great-grandchildren. She is loving, affectionate, communicative, smart, fun, funny, and she is my best friend.

I am the second oldest of five children. I have one older sister (just don't remind her she is *older*), two younger sisters that happen to be identical twins born on Valentine's Day, and we have a baby brother, who at 37, is not much of a baby anymore. He is adopted and my parents say it was the only way they were going to get a boy after four girls. Both of my parents always worked full-time to support us. My dad worked full-time as a policeman and also had to work second jobs to help make ends meet. My mother worked as a teller, and then at an accounting firm and, finally, she began her own accounting business. My parents were very young when they fell in love and married. My mom was 16 and my dad was 22 and he jokes that he had to sign her report cards because she was still in high school when they married.

My mother taught me everything about being a woman, a friend and a mother. I hear her voice when I talk with my children, I called her when I was a new mother to ask advice and cry on her shoulder when my adopted son had night terrors. I could call her anytime when my daughter was going through 5 ½ months of colic. I can and have called her day or night to talk, to cry, to vent, or just to say hi.

I had never been able to have children and my Mom always teased me that I would become pregnant when I was forty. Well, in August of 2003 at the age of 41 ½, I became pregnant. I took two pregnancy tests, both instantly positive, and then called my Mom right away. I was still walking around in shock after the doctor confirmed the pregnancy and my Mom was already shopping for material to make all of my maternity clothes. My Mom was there for me throughout my pregnancy. She accompanied me to most of my OB appointments, watched every sonogram, and cried when she heard the heartbeat. She even threw an amazing baby shower for me. She was standing outside of the operating room when my daughter was born via C-section on April 8, 2004, which was also my parent's 51st wedding anniversary. My mother and my daughter have an amazing bond. They are so close and when my daughter and I visit my daughter likes to sit on her lap and have conversations with her NANA. They have this look that they share that is much more than love; it is a knowing look of an unbreakable bond.

My mother was diagnosed with breast cancer in 2007 and went through an extensive radiology treatment program. She was in pain, she was burned, and she was scared but she did every treatment with a smile. Every amount of discomfort she went through was endured with a smile or a laugh. Her whole demeanor was awe inspiring. She continued to work even when she was in pain. She continued to ask about, worry about, and remain involved with her children, grand-children and great-grandchildren. She never wavered in her belief that she would be cured and, as I write this, the reports have all been very positive. She worried about her four daughters getting mammograms, which we all did, and so far so good. All of this was while she was going through possibly the worst health scare of her life. She is an amazing, strong, loving, caring woman, who always puts her family first and I truly would be lost without her. I speak with her every day, I listen to her, I see her as often as possible, and I spend time with her. She is my best friend, my confidante, my precious, treasured angel. I hope someday, when my daughter is grown, she and I will have a relationship as strong and as solid as mine is with my mother.

Her strength and her belief in me has inspired me to achieve many of my goals in life like earning my MBA, being a successful single mom and having the faith in myself to strive to always reach for the stars, never give up, and always try to do better.

I hope my story has inspired readers to thank their mothers or mother figures for being there and for contributing to who they are and who they may become.

Tami
Social work professional, mother

My mother was born on October 30, 1952 as Suzanne Catherine. She was the middle child, with one sister who was four years older and another who was 14 years younger. She was raised in a valley in Pennsylvania called Wyoming Valley. This is also where she met my father. She had recently ended an engagement with her long term boyfriend and had vowed she didn't want to get married. That is of course until she met my father and fell madly in love. She knew almost instantly that she would spend the rest of her life with him. So, at the age of 24, she got married. My mother had worked in the insurance business with her mother and had taken a few classes at the local community college before meeting my father. She gave birth to twins a year and a half after marriage and stayed home with us until we were five years old. My fathers' health was failing and she needed to go back to work so she did what she knew best and went back into the insurance business.

My parents' marriage is very loving. They truly care about each other and what the other thinks. I believe that this set a very high standard of what I expected out of marriage. I wanted a husband who was caring and loving and I also wanted to make sure that his needs are met. My parents would have their fights like normal people but they would never resort to name calling or belittling each other; they would just argue over what the situation was. I believe that taught me a lot, too.

My parents had twins on their first try which was perfect for them. My father had his daughter and my mother had her son. It never bothered me that growing up she favored my brother because my relationship with my father was so strong that I never felt like I was missing anything. She never treated me poorly but just felt that she had to defend my brother because he was always in trouble. This was usually his own fault.

My mother is a loving, caring individual with a great sense of humor and a great sense of loyalty. She is a woman who will give you the shirt off her back and what ever is in the refrigerator along with it. I have always admired my mothers' sense of giving. She is a pleaser. She wants to keep the peace. I remember that I would watch my mother give everything she had to everyone and have nothing left for herself. I knew that I would also be a pleaser but I always wanted to make sure to take care of myself too. I also admired my mothers' love for her family. She was there to help with her aging grandmothers even though she worked a full time job and was raising two kids. She would take her grandmothers shopping at Christmas time or go to their house to wash their hair. My mother is a role model when it comes to a loving spirit. She loves people so deeply and always wants those people to happy. I learned by watching her how to truly care for people. My mothers' parenting style was, as we affectionately referred to her, "the lawyer". My parents would show a united front when it came to parenting, although my father was the stricter parent. So, if we wanted to get off grounding or have a special favor we would go to our "lawyer" and she would negotiate the details for us. Interestingly enough she never charged us.

I believe a lesson that I have learned from my mother about being a mother is that you should always put your family first. That will not always be an easy decision but it is worth it in the end. Friends, job, etc., come and go but your family is always your family.

As I was growing up my mothers' approval was very important. I wanted to make her proud, which luckily for me was an easy thing to do. Throughout most of my life I made choices that made my mother proud. When I was an adult and met my husband I made a decision that, at the time, was against my mothers' wishes. It hurt me to go against her and my father but I knew that I was justified in my decision making. At that point in my life I pulled away from pleasing my mother (and father) and made the decision that I felt was best for me. From that point on the decisions I make are for my best interest and not to please anyone else.

My relationship with my mother now is that of a deep friendship. We do not blur the lines of who is the mother and who is the daughter. We confide in each other and vent about our husbands and in-laws. She is the first person I call when I am upset or mad or extremely happy or excited. She has a way of calming me down like none other. We talk to each other an average of 4 times a day, but usually more than that. Most would think that is excessive but not for us. She has a way of being connected in my life without interfering or controlling it. I feel blessed to have my mother in my life.

Heather
Social Services professional, wife, mother

L.L.

Section V

Respect, admiration and friendship....

Camille

Emily

Monetta

Cathy

Lin

Lynda

Family faces are magic mirrors. Looking at people who belong to us, we see the past, present and future.

~Gail Lumet Buckley

My mother was born in 1912 in Nebraska. She was the oldest of four children, with three younger brothers. After she graduated from high school, Mom worked in a bank until she was married in 1933 at the age of 21. After they were married Dad went in the service and Mom stayed behind to care for her mother, who was in poor health. She lived in Nebraska until after my father got out of the service and was offered a job opportunity in Colorado. By the time they moved to Colorado they had my sister. I was a big surprise, born when my sister was 13 and my parents had given up the idea of being able to have more children!

My parents had a very good marriage. They were respectful of each other and loved each other deeply. If they had any disagreements it must have been in private because I was never aware of them. They were very compatible and showed me a great example of what a marriage should be. They treated each other well and were very good to us girls. I have often wondered why I have been unable to find that in my own life when I had such a good role model. I didn't consciously look for a man like my father to marry but I know I expected to have a marriage similar to my parents. When I got married I was fully committed to making it work. In hindsight, I think maybe I was so committed to the marriage that I wouldn't allow myself to admit that it wasn't going to work. After ten years and 3 children, I finally had to admit to myself that the marriage couldn't be saved, which was one of the hardest decisions I have ever made.

I would describe Mom as a dominant, strong-willed, and probably controlling person who has never had a problem speaking her mind. I have to say she is a "what you see is what you get" type of person. She has always had a tendency to exaggerate and turn situations into more of a drama than they actually are. Mom has always been a social person and I think because my Dad was a traveling salesman for many years she developed a lot of her own interests and friendships. She is the type of person who can strike up a conversation with anyone – no one is a stranger to my Mom. She has a curious mind and is always asking questions and trying to analyze things. My Mom is a very positive person with strong faith and she has always said that there is a “silver lining” to any problem or hard time. I think I got that from her because I am usually the same way and have been like that with my daughters.

I think your basic personality has a lot to do with how you turn out but I’m a very independent person and I think I learned that from my Mom because she is independent and self-sufficient. Even though my parents had a close relationship, she didn’t lose her identity. That is an important thing about being a woman that I learned from her because, as important as my marriage was to me, I think I always kept a sense of myself. When I was a single parent, raising 3 girls on my own, I knew I could have asked my parents for help at any time but I never did because I wanted to be an independent adult.

An important thing I learned from my Mom about being a mother is to believe in your children and always let them know you love them. My mother isn’t a sweet and gentle type but I always knew I was loved. One way I tried to be different than her with my children is that I try not to interfere in their lives. I think Mom interfered too much with me and my sister because she tends to be controlling.

I have always had a good relationship with my mother but, as we have gotten older, I think we have become good friends and we have grown even closer. After my sister died I felt a strong sense of obligation to fill in the void that her death left in Mom’s life.

I can relate the phrase “velvet ropes” to my relationship with my mother because I definitely feel emotionally bound to her but not in a way that hurts me. I also think of the rope as a life line because I have always been able to talk to her about anything.

Camille
Retired business professional, mother, grandmother

My Mom, Catherine Ann, was born in Manitowoc, WI on December 17, 1946 to Sara Catherine and Richard. It is important to note that although she was born in Wisconsin, she was conceived in Dade City, Florida - this is a critical detail in which her maternal grandmother ("Granny Mac") found great comfort as a means of confirming my mother's Southern roots. God forbid her beloved firstborn granddaughter be a Yankee! The weather and the distance from Granny Mac proved too much to bear, so the family moved back to Florida shortly after Ms. Catherine Ann was born. For four glorious years, Cathy was the queen bee of the household. Right about that time, her brother Andrew ("Andy") was born. Once he could begin to walk, he was following her around and taking orders. Cathy was loving but directive as an older sis...a trait that carries forth to this day.

With respect to her marriage to my Dad, I'm certain it did influence my love relationships. They had a profound love and respect for each other as people and as partners. They often referred to each other as "co-conspirators," a notion that I thoroughly love. They both were strong advocates for each other, and sometimes great critics; however, never critical in public. Certainly my father's brain tumor intensified their relationship, but I think it was for the better. They learned not to be careless with their time together. I know that is a theme in my relationships. I don't want to waste time with people in whom I am not invested. Consequently, my intimate group is quite small but deep. It has engendered this "fierce urgency of now," that can be a little heavy at times. I think I expect to be treated with respect, acceptance and adoration in my relationships because of the model that was presented to me. I also think I look for people who will push me to be better. I've never looked for people that I can save or change; I am drawn to men with strength of character and an inner knowledge of themselves. And, of course, humor is absolutely a requirement. One of the things that my parents definitely showed me was how to laugh, which is pretty remarkable considering all of the heavy life and death stuff that we were living through. I really hit the lottery when it comes to the parents I got.

This is an interesting exercise - to examine the woman who has literally been with me from the beginning and is absolutely a part of me and who I am. The words are difficult to find because our relationship transcends words. I know it when I feel it and how do I describe that? Let me give you an example:

For the majority of my youth, my mother was perfect. She could do no wrong. In fact, she lived in this bubble of perfection that made her infallible – even when there were glaring faults. I had total acceptance and awe. It was not until I was 16 did I even suspect that she might be human and flawed. In this year, one major event tested the fortitude of our relationship.

It was early May of 1990 when a friend had a mother-daughter tea to celebrate her Sweet Sixteen. There were about 18 pairs of mothers and daughters lunching at a very swanky restaurant on the Westside of Los Angeles. At the end of the meal, my friend began to open her presents, getting the customary "oohs" and "aahs" from her guests. There was however one voice that resonated above the others – that of my mother's intoxicated voice. Apparently, wine had been flowing at the table where the mothers were sitting and my Mom's glass did not have a bottom. Mom's voice grew louder with each present that was opened and I kept wondering why it took so long to unwrap the damned presents. Why did she have to be so careful not to tear the paper? Why did she have to spend so much time fawning over the engraved silver key chain? For the love of God, just rip open the packages and be done with it!

As the unwrapping continued, I breathed a sigh of relief when Mom excused herself from the table to go to the restroom. Unfortunately, the worse was yet to come. About 2 minutes after

Mom excused herself, a waiter came back to the luncheon room to get the attention of one of the other mothers. She went with the waiter and very quickly came back to get me. I don't recall whose mother she was but fortunately she was very discrete. Apparently, my Mom had been throwing up in the bathroom and couldn't stand up. The wine had betrayed her; she had betrayed me. All the wise minds involved felt that it might be a good time to leave (and me without any cake!).

At that moment, I lost all sympathy for Mom. The bubble burst. How could she do this to me? I was burning inside. My heart was beating furiously; my jaw, clenched in anger, rendering me unable to speak. Please let me disappear from here. The drive home was silent, allowing my rage to build as I replayed every frame of the afternoon. Up to this point, her mistakes had been hers alone...at least in my recollection. This time I got dragged under the bus with her. This event had the potential to destroy my trust in her - it certainly chinked the armor - and the reason it didn't destroy our trust is one of her great teachings to me. She let me be alone in my anger without pushing on me any justification or rationalization or spin for her behavior. In the time that I was processing everything, she wrote me a note. Again, she did not try to explain away what she had done or minimize it. Instead, she acknowledged my feelings, accepted responsibility for her actions, apologized, and asked for forgiveness. We were reciprocal. I was to be her soft place to land just like all the times that she had been mine. She trusted me enough to bestow on me that responsibility. I think all the time I held her up as perfection I missed the beauty and detail of her humanity; the parts of her that make her accessible and vulnerable and the parts that show me how to forgive my own imperfections. I still have the note that she wrote me. I read it occasionally, crying whenever I do.

As I reflect on that story, I am now better able to fill in the context - Dad was battling brain cancer, my sister was struggling with where she belonged, I was struggling with where I belonged, my Mom was the sole financial and emotional support for the family. There was so much pressure on her to keep it together. I think all of the other mothers at the luncheon could see that because nothing was ever mentioned to me. In fact, I never heard about it again.

Our relationship has continued to evolve as I've matured and as we've shared more experiences. My Dad died two years after the "Los Angeles Tea Party". In those two years there were surgeries and recoveries and realities that we had to face. Because she allowed me to really see her, we were able to support one another in a mutually beneficial way.

My Mom is an extremely accomplished woman. She is successful in business, in the community, in relationships and in family. Anything she touches becomes gold. It is because she gives her gifts so freely that she is a light in this life. I am reminded of her when I hear that bible song – “this little light of mine, I'm gonna let it shine, let it shine, let it shine, let it shine”.

I am not a mother or a wife but I am a daughter and a strong woman. I am still finding my way - perhaps, more slowly than my Mom would like - examining my life, almost ad nauseum, so as not to take for granted the gifts I have been given. It is extremely important that my Mom holds me in high esteem, and so I do all that I can to make sure that she does. The paradox; however, is that I could do nothing of which she approved and she would love me just the same. I know that.

What she is....

My mother is a life force, a magnet - strong, powerful, and attractive.

She is generous, though not frivolous, with her spirit, time, and material resources.

She is complex, yet often speaks in bumper stickers.

She can make me laugh when I want to cry and will let me cry when I need to cry.

She is mischievous and silly.

She is resilient without being tough.

She is brilliant in the ways of things that matter.

She is optimistic and bold.

She is the cyber queen.

She asks why *and* why not.

She embraces a philosophy of abundance.

What she is to me....

She is my guide, my cheerleader, my friend, my teacher, my student, my sounding board, my soft place to land, my lighter side.

She is my MAMA.

Emily
Human BE-ing,

My mother, Desiree Ann, was born on October 16, 1948 in British Guiana. She was the oldest of 9 children (7 girls and 2 boys) born to Curtis and Mavis. Psychological profiles usually show that the oldest child is bossy and controlling of younger siblings but I definitely do not think this profile fits my Mum. As the oldest of so many siblings my Mum's role and personality were defined at an early age and, to this day, she is regarded as the peacemaker or the "neutral" one in the family. I like to call her the diplomat. She is the one who maintains the peace if there is discord between any of the sisters by listening to all sides and helping each to see the other's point of view. And as a mother, she applies the same tactic when dealing with any disagreement between my sisters and me.

My Mum lived a very sheltered life; a direct result of having a very strict father, and she was certainly the good child who never got into trouble. As a child she enjoyed reading and socializing and learning many practical skills as a Brownie and a Girl Guide. During high school she was the typical teenage girl of her time who enjoyed listening to Elvis Presley and the Beatles. She also developed an appreciation for classical music and instrumental jazz. After high school my Mum started working as a public servant at one of the government run agencies. She also enrolled part-time at the University of Guiana where she majored in English with a minor in French. In 1969 she met my father, Owen, a young civil engineer who attended a birthday party, uninvited, for a chance to meet her. Within just a few months of courting he asked her to marry him. She accepted, with her father's permission, of course, and they were married a year and a half later on April 3, 1971, just six months shy of her 23rd birthday. After she married my Dad, Mum continued to work and also with her studies at the university; however, 3 months into their marriage she became pregnant and I was born on April 25, 1972.

After years of being like a second mother to her younger siblings, I don't believe the reality of becoming a mother to her own child was exactly what my mother expected. She was now responsible for a new baby and her husband's expectations of her role had shifted. My Dad wanted my Mum to become a full time mother and wife, giving up her career and university studies; however, my grandmother, a stay-at-home mother, had passed down a credo to her daughters.....*they should always earn their own money and never depend on a man to buy them everything.* My mother in turn passed this credo down to her own daughters. Eventually, my mother did agree to abandon her studies but she went back to work six weeks after I was born. My mother was uneasy about strangers taking care of me and so a wonderful relative, Auntie Beryl, who I consider my second mother, came to live with us and help to raise me, and later my sisters, for nine years.

Alas, my mother was 24 years old and her best friends were still single and free. She missed being able to join their social gatherings on a whim and, when I was a year old, she decided to join them on a 10 week vacation to Jamaica, Canada, and the United States. She had a great holiday but, when she returned home, her baby did not know her and had started to call Auntie Beryl "Mummy". My mother told me that she was devastated but it was this incident that re-defined and developed a newfound appreciation of her role as a mother. In six years my Mum had two more daughters and, after her third child was born, she went back to university and eventually received a degree in public administration. Shortly thereafter she started another degree program in business administration.

My early teenage years were challenging for my mother. By that time my grandparents and all of my mother's siblings had immigrated to America. My Mum's familial support system was gone. I remember reading a letter from my grandmother to my mother, asking her to be patient with me and saying that I was just going through a phase. In retrospect, I think Mum would agree that I was not really a bad kid but, I was a defiant and stubborn kid who was also a bit mouthy. In my mind I was always right and Mum was always wrong. She would probably say today that I haven't changed much in this regard.

I was resentful of my Mum because she was not a "regular" mother. While she made us every breakfast and weekend meal (during the week we had lunch with Dad's mother, Granny Edith, and dinner at Auntie Beryl's), got us ready for school, helped us with our homework, sang bedtime songs to us (mine was *Golden Slumber*), and on Saturday afternoons she took us to get our usual treat of ice cream and pizza at *Demico,* a local fast food restaurant, in my eyes she was still not a "good enough" mother. My Mum was a university trained career woman, she was not the stay-at-home mum who welcomed her kids every afternoon with a home cooked meal, and she did not bake cookies and scones with us. *That* mum was the ideal to me since that was the reality of the majority of my friends. Years later, as an adult, I spoke with one of those friends and she told me how much she admired my mother and many of the reasons she admired her were the exact reasons that made me resentful of the kind of mother she was. It was in that moment that I really evaluated the woman who is my mother and the woman that I had become and it became clear to me that my strong, confident, and independent character was a direct result of being raised by a woman of the same character. That is when I think I had the *"a-ha"* moment and was extremely proud of my mother. Sometimes it bothers me that it took my friend's admission of the admiration she had for my mother to make me realize that but I tell myself that it was a latent feeling that I always had.

In 1988 my Mum made a significant sacrifice for her children. My aunts in the United States suggested that they allow me and my younger sister to move to the US. They reasoned that, at ages 13 and 16, it would be a perfect time for us to enter the

American school system and thus allow us an easier transition later on into the university system. It was a difficult decision for Mum as she would be breaking up our family but she conceded that it was the right move and, together with my Dad, agreed to it. So, on December 17, 1988, my mother, my two sisters and I made the journey to Rochester, NY, to join my grandparents, aunts, uncles, and cousins. My Dad followed a few days later. My parents enrolled my sister and me in middle and high school, respectively, for the January semester. They made a last minute decision to allow our baby sister to stay because she didn't want to go back to Guiana without us. My Dad was running a company that managed the contracts on civil works for governmental and private industries in the country; Mum was steadily rising through the ranks of management at her company and just a year and a half away from completing her business administration degree. But, in all of this, there was sadness. In Guiana my mother struggled with being away from her children and in the US her children, especially the two younger ones, were missing her immensely. It was usually with great anticipation that we waited for the Saturday morning call from her. After much crying and pleading from my younger sisters, Mum finally decided to join us in the US and arrived in August 1989. She resigned from her job and gave up her studies, now just less than a year before she would attain the degree. But, most of all, my parents made the ultimate sacrifice to live in two different countries as my father felt that he would be more able to support his family if he remained in Guiana. By the way, 21 years later my parents still live apart but my Dad has religiously made the journey to Rochester 2-3 times every year.

Settling into a good life in the US was mixed for my mother. While she was finally with her children and had the familial support group, things socially and economically were drastically different for her. She had gone from having a very active social life in Guiana, a married woman living a very comfortable life and at the height of her career to having to basically start her life over in the US. She and her husband were living in different countries, she and her three girls were living in a rented 2 bedroom apartment, and she was doing temp work at a variety of businesses. She no longer had an active social life or the need for a new party dress every other month or so. Her life revolved around her children and family, and the current temp job. But, my Mum was a resilient woman and she knew that she had to be there for her children physically, emotionally, and financially. She had a strong work ethic and one of the companies where she temped requested through an agency that she interview with them for a permanent position. Mum was hired in August 1990 and was with the company for the next 20 years.

My Mum accomplished a lot. She completed her business administration degree and attained several promotions within her company. She enjoys going to the theater and has steadily built a social circle of girlfriends, though most of her socializing is still with her sisters at the weekly Saturday and Sunday night gatherings at my grandparent's house. She has put three daughters through college and two have gone on to achieve master's degrees. She thinks her life is complete except for the grandchildren for which she yearns.

My mother is a mother and friend to her daughters. I would say the friend aspect didn't develop until we were no longer her dependents, as her only role was as a mother before then. All three of us call her about 5-6 times a week and I dare say there are weeks when we chat everyday! My mother instilled so many good values in us. We were raised not to be materialistic and at a very early age she encouraged s to be charitable to those less fortunate. We were never the type of kids who saw something on TV or in the supermarket aisle and demanded to have it or throw tantrums when we were told no. We were brought up to appreciate what was given to us and not want more. We were raised to be tolerant and accepting of everyone regardless of class (Guiana is a mostly class conscious society), race, or orientation.

My relationship through the years with my mother endured the ups and downs of most relationships between mothers and daughters. As an adult some issues do creep up. For instance, Mum might make the odd snide remark about my weight or would offer some unsolicited advice, or I may get upset with her terrible habit of procrastinating or her less than perfect money management skills but I have learned through the years to just accept that this is her. As a result, I have been able to nurture my relationship with my mother and harbor no resentment towards her, especially in these instances. She is my Mum and I will always respect her opinions and behaviors, whether I agree with them or not.

My mother is a woman of integrity, a woman who is kind and fair, and, most importantly, the woman who is the best mother she can be to me and my sisters. I respect and admire the choices she has made in her life. They may not have been the choices of some or choices I agreed with at the time but, they were the choices that were right for her. Our lives have not mirrored each other. I did not get married and start a family in my twenties; instead I am in my late thirties, unmarried and childless. I completed my bachelor's and master's degrees right after high school and have built a career since then.

Many people tell me that I am like my mother. Is that a compliment or not? Usually when my sisters say it to me it is with a negative connotation if they perceive that I am nagging them about something. Nevertheless, negative connotation or not, there is no doubt that I aspire to be like my Mum. I am pretty sure that if I ever have a daughter I will mother her almost exactly like my Mum mothered me.

In the end, the values that my mother has instilled in me through the years will be the same ones that I would instill in my daughter, should I be so lucky to have one.

Monetta
Event Planner, daughter, sister

Mama was born Sara Catherine on December 15, 1921 to Charles and Catherine of Dade City, Florida. She joined her brother, Charles, four years her senior, and they lived in a house built for my grandparents by my great and great-great grandfathers.

To understand how my mother lived I need to tell how she died. My dear sweet Mama died on August 16, 2003 at nearly 82 years of age. She had been a bride for 60 years, having just celebrated that milestone with her beloved Rich on August 8, 2003. Not one day in all that time did her eyes fail to light up just being in his presence and it was reciprocal.

Just two months earlier she had gall bladder surgery, or so we thought. The surgery revealed the horror of cancer everywhere. She called from the hospital with the news. When I answered the phone her hearty voice said, “Well, the jig is up”. Panic raged through my body, tears consumed me, and I could barely speak. Yet she kept on, in a spirited way, as if to describe a new journey she would take. It is still a blur to recall the details; yet I remember clearly her voice, and tears flow down my cheeks as I recall that moment. It was typical Mama; my Mama. Spirited, supremely optimistic, uniquely able to put the best construction on any circumstance. Her glass was not just half full; it stayed full.

My high school chum is the head nurse at the hospital where Mama was being treated. Calls to her confirmed the worst. Plans were made to go to her. Mama’s wish was that we proceed with the long planned 60th anniversary party. She had delighted in anticipating the event for the prior year. My brother and I hosted the party, along with her adoring granddaughters. She was surrounded by everyone she loved. She looked like a million bucks, even though she had to resort to using a wheelchair. She was the Queen Bee with her beloved Rich at her side.

She died at home, surrounded by her family. She had received a steady stream of visitors and she was the one who comforted them. Her wish was to remain in the home that had been her refuge, which she and my father built together in 1950. We were all devoted to assuring that result.

My grandmother, Catherine, was a formidable figure. She attended Florida State College for Women, now FSU, when such a thing was extremely rare. By all accounts, she was a brain and a beauty. She married the love of her life, Herbert, in 1914 and they began their life together in Island Grove, Florida, where he was the school principal. Their dreams were extinguished a year later when Herbert died of influenza and Catherine returned to her parents in Dade City.

Catherine worked at the local bank and that is where she met the dashing Charles. Tall, handsome and very dynamic, he was in town helping to build roads. They had a whirlwind romance and, against the backdrop of World War I, they were married in 1916. Catherine was thrilled for this second chance at happiness and to begin her own family but, this was not to be.

The generational pull goes back another generation to Catherine's mother, Annie Elizabeth, the matriarch of the family. Annie Elizabeth was never quite comfortable with the charming stranger who had captured her daughter's affections. Annie Elizabeth was a virtual pillar of Dade City society and arbiter of standards and propriety. Charles, as they say, "was not from here". Over the years it has turned into legend but it seems that Charles drank alcohol and smoked, which shocked Annie Elizabeth's sensibilities. When he wrote a check that was returned for insufficient funds he lost all credibility in her eyes. She pressed her daughter to separate from this wanton man and then to divorce him. By her standards that was preferred to any association with such a scoundrel, regardless of the fact that there were two babies to be raised by her daughter! (There has to be more to this but this is the story that has been passed down!)

Annie Elizabeth's will prevailed and Catherine divorced her husband and began the life of a single parent; however, she did live across the street from her parents, who pitched in to help with raising my uncle and mother. And there were other assorted aunts and uncles and cousins. In this milieu my mother developed a deep devotion to family and duty and the importance of attending to the needs of others. This is the backdrop of my mother's growing up. Her older brother, Charles, was the one upon whom my grandmother pinned her hopes and he did not disappoint, rising to Colonel in the Army and later Dean of the Graduate School of Business at Syracuse University. His major failing was in finding a Yankee wife during WWII.

Mama clearly understood her role model! She excelled in school and was editor of the paper and captain of the basketball team in high school. She graduated from Florida State College for Women and came home to teach high school in Dade City. WWII was a fact of her young life and at a dance for the soldiers stationed near Dade City she met my father. To hear them both tell the story, it was love at first sight. Perhaps, in those dramatic times, the circumstances created a different level of urgency. Whatever, there was no turning back for either of them.

They married in August 1943. Daddy was immediately shipped to Europe where he was part of the Normandy invasion. Mama wrote letters everyday and she kept them all, which is a treasure for me. He came home in 1945. After trying out Dade City and my father's home state of Wisconsin, they began their lives together in Largo, Florida, when I was two.

My memories of my mother are so intertwined with memories of my father. Theirs was a true partnership long before that sort of egalitarian model was the norm. Mama always worked because she wanted to. Daddy would have preferred that she had stayed home in the mode of that era but she would not be dissuaded. Mama worked as a caseworker for the Department of Public Welfare. Daddy worked as a lineman for Florida Power Company. That post WWII period in Florida was a boom time yet Florida was still a very poor state at that time. They both had what were considered "good jobs" since many others had more seasonal work. I can think of no time that I ever felt we did not have enough or that I was insecure in any way about my future. That "living with a safety net" is a theme in my own life, giving me confidence to boldly move in any direction I chose.

For me, my parents' marriage was a hallmark for what marriage ought to be. They were partners, lovers, and friends. They were considerate of each other and they were champions of each other. They were the universal "we". My mother was the dominant personality. She never met a stranger. Her level of vibration was high and influenced all around her. Things just felt better when she was around.

My mother taught me that you are both entitled and obligated to choose your own path. She knew exactly what she wanted and never deviated from that. She wanted no less for me. My first "big decision" was in choosing to work for the American Red Cross in South Vietnam in 1968. The war was raging and it would have been easy for her to say no. Instead, she said she believed in me and would support whatever I wished to do. As a mother, I now know that was not an easy statement for her to make. And so, I left for a one year tour of duty at the height of the Vietnam War. It was a good decision. My parents did not reveal any consternation to me about that decision.

As a role model, my mother taught me that women rule. I know that sounds crass, but that was her point of view and it filtered to me. As part of that she knew that women were essential in the world of companionship and as hospitality facilitators because when men are left to their own devices the world is a bleak place indeed.

As a child there was no other point of view than that of my mother. If she said it, it must be so. As a young adult I took exception to some of her edicts. She had her point of view and I had mine. Her approval meant the world to me, but the great irony is that she taught me to live independent of other people's good opinion of me. She was grounded in the notion of doing the next right thing. She invented the idea that "all people behave in ways that make sense to them". This gave her cover in observing the many different ways that people behave.

We were physically different as I grew up. I had my father's red hair. I was compact and short and she was tall. She had the dark hair of her father and the more prominent features that his pictures reveal. Yet, when people engaged us both together they would always comment on how much we looked alike. That always confounded me until much later. For it was then that I understood how one spirit can imprint another. My mother and I are deeply imprinted. We talk alike, we laugh alike. We are embedded in each other. We do not possess "velvet ropes". We possess the same DNA. We are inextricably connected at a level beyond my understanding. I am she in so many ways. I am honored to have been her daughter and I only hope my daughters can feel some of what this means to me. I miss her every day yet I am energized by her spirit. I feel a sense of invulnerability; she is my talisman.

Catherine
Non-profit executive director, wife, mother, grandmother

My mother, Belle, was born in 1916 in Brooklyn, NY. She was the middle child of two girls and two boys. She attended Manhattan College and worked as a secretary for an attorney before she got married at the age of 26. She also helped out at her brother's restaurant at times.

My parents were from two totally different backgrounds. My mother was Jewish and my father was Italian Catholic and they were raised very differently. They had very different view points on all kinds of subjects, especially when it came to how and what my father should do for a living. My mother was very vocal and my father was so good natured that he never wanted to "make waves". It was obvious that they cared for and respected each other very much and they demonstrated it in many ways.

For most of my life I was my mother's favorite, especially as an adult. I felt very protective of my younger sister and brother and had an amazing sense of responsibility that still carries over to this day.

My mother was an "Auntie Mame"; outgoing, gregarious, loving, caring, affectionate, funny - wonderful. I consider myself to be an independent woman and that is what my mother was. When I got married it was to someone who reminded me of my father in a lot of different areas: respectful, protective of his family, funny, intelligent and a little reserved.

Lessons I learned from her about being a woman: be independent, family comes first, stand up for yourself, don't let people walk over you. That is how she lived her life. Lessons I learned from her about being a mother: love, love, love your children and try to give them a good upbringing. Morals, ethics, responsibility.

I tried not to be as much of a disciplinarian as my mother and I taught my daughter she could be anything she wanted to be. When I was growing up there was a different mindset as far as what a woman could become. Basically a teacher, nurse or secretary. The options were not as broad as they are now.

My mother was killed in a car accident more than 20 years ago and I still think of her every day! We were friends aside from having a mother/daughter relationship. She meant so much to me and I still wish she was here to share my family and our lives. As she got older she became more rigid in her thinking and actions and sometimes that caused friction but it did not occur very often. We spoke every day and I knew she loved me very much. The feeling was mutual.

My mother's approval was extremely important to me even as an adult. She supported most of my decisions, especially when it came to how I was raising my children. She was very proud of me and the work I was doing and I always strived to do well.

There is a special connection between mothers and daughters that almost cannot be explained. Most of the women I know love and respect their mothers. Of course there are many that do not have a good relationship with their mothers but when all is said and done your mother is tied to you from birth. The caring, the worry, the excitement, joy, happiness, sleepless nights, the "talks", the sharing, the feeling of sisterhood as a daughter grows up and becomes an adult, the tears and laughter but most of all the love, that is what binds us.

Lin
Non-profit executive director, mother, grandmother

My Mom, Brenda, was born in Harrogate, Yorkshire, England on April 11, 1929. Mom was the second of seven children, two boys and five girls, born to Albert Henry and Muriel "Molly". Mom grew up during the Depression and World War II and has very clear memories of food rationing, blackout curtains on the windows, people being unemployed for years, soup lines, and families that were evacuated from London to escape the German bombs. In those days working class children in England were finished with school at the age of 14 and went to work. The girls usually worked in shops, factories, or offices and the boys would often go into apprenticeship to learn a trade. Very few families were able to send their children for higher education.

When she finished school Mom went to work in a shop and, in addition to turning most of her wages over to her mother, she was expected to help out with household chores and caring for her younger siblings. She loved to dance and, at one time, had dreams of becoming a dance instructor. She didn't have a close relationship with her mother, who was high strung and quick tempered. Mom felt she never had any privacy or respect for her belongings. Many years later the feelings were still fresh when she recalled how her mother opened a package that was sent to her from the family of a Canadian airman, whose grave Mom tended, and the items were distributed among the younger siblings before she got home from work. At the age of 18, she met my father. He was 24 and had recently returned home after serving in the Royal Air Force in India during World War II. The way Mom describes it, there was an immediate attraction between them and she said that she knew right away that he was "the one" for her. She once told me that when she looked in his eyes she saw her future.

Mom and Dad got married on July 23, 1949 and I was born on November 25, 1950. They wanted to have a large family but, as things worked out, I was an only child. I have often thought that it would have been better for my Mom if she could have had more than one child on whom to focus her love and strong maternal instincts.

When I was five my parents immigrated to the United States. My Mom's parents and all her siblings had already immigrated at the encouragement of her older sister, who had married an American GI from New Jersey, and my Mom missed them terribly. Our first year in this country was spent at my grandparents' house, along with the four of my Mom's siblings who were still living at home. For that year both my parents worked and saved every dollar they could spare to buy a house and, after we moved into our own house, Mom quit her job and went back to being a full time mother and homemaker. My parents agreed that they wanted my Mom to be a stay at home mother even though it would have been much easier for them financially if she had gone out to work. They both felt that my care and upbringing was more important than anything else.

My parents had what I think of as a traditional, old-fashioned marriage. They had clearly defined roles – he was the "breadwinner" and she was the mother and "homemaker" – but they were equals within the relationship and always made decisions together. After my Dad started his own electrical contracting business she became his secretary/bookkeeper. As a teenager and young woman, I misunderstood their relationship. At the time the Women's Liberation movement was in full swing and I thought my Mom was subservient to my Dad because she waited on him "hand and foot". I didn't understand that they each felt that their contributions to the partnership were important and equal. Her role as a wife and mother defined her in many ways.

I wish I had understood and appreciated my parent's relationship better when I was younger because I think I might have made better choices in my own relationships if I had. I didn't fully appreciate the respect, trust, and love they had for each other until I was well into my 40's. My parents both had a good sense of humor and had a lot of fun together. They also worked together as a team – they never pulled in different directions and I rarely heard them fight about anything. In the end, I think what I finally learned about relationships from them is that there is nothing more important than respect and trust – and that actions are always more important than words.

My Mom was a tomboy as a child. I think, as she grew up, she continued to prefer the company of men over women. I have often heard her say that she doesn't like to be with a bunch of "cackling" women and I think she has always found it difficult to trust women or to feel close to them. As a result, I have not known her to have many friends. She is one of the least vain women I have ever known and can't be bothered fussing with her hair or makeup. She was never the type to get a manicure or facial but I always thought she was prettier than any of my friend's mothers.

She has always been very talented with all types of handiwork – sewing, crocheting, knitting, embroidery, needlepoint, sewing, macramé – and she taught herself all those skills. She is also a talented baker. She has a natural mechanical ability and can usually figure out how to fix anything. She has always underplayed her talents and tends to shrug off compliments. She encouraged my creativity and has always been my biggest fan. Throughout my childhood she made all my clothes and even made tiny outfits for my Barbie dolls. When I entered junior high I wanted "store bought" clothes like my friends. It didn't take long for me to realize that, not only was the quality of the clothes she made for me better than anything I could buy but, I could design them myself! We had a lot of fun shopping for material and modifying patterns to fit some new design I had created.

It is hard for me to describe my Mom's personality because there are many times when I don't understand her. She has always encouraged me to express my feelings but she doesn't do that herself so sometimes her reactions to situations are a mystery to me. She is friendly to people but doesn't "make friends" with them even though she has always encouraged me to be social and have friends. She doesn't open up to people or trust easily. She has a strong sense of herself and what she thinks is right and wrong but, sometimes, this comes across to me as being judgmental or overly critical. I think one of our main personality differences is that Mom tends to see things only as black or white, good or bad, whereas, I see a lot more shades of gray. There have been many times when I wished I could be as sure of everything as she seems to be. I have the same independent nature as her but, as a young woman I had a tendency to be insecure and crave approval, which is definitely not like her! I realize now that she taught me, not so much with words but more by example, how to be a strong woman who knows her own mind. It's not her fault that it took me so long to learn the lesson!

Mom and I have always had a close relationship and enjoyed spending time together although we had our share of conflict as I was growing up. We were sometimes at odds with each other when I was an adolescent and teenager, mainly because I didn't want to be controlled by her, but even during those years we were always able to have fun and laugh together. I don't think I really grew up completely until I moved 1,200 miles away from my parents when I was 43 and started a new life in Florida with no one to rely on but myself. By the time my father retired and my parents moved near me I felt that I was a successful, independent, mature woman in my own right and I was able to have a true adult relationship with them. Since my father passed away I see my Mom a lot more often and I am grateful that we enjoy each other's company and that I am able to give something back to her because she has given me so much.

I'm sure I learned a lot about how to be a mother from my Mom but my life was very different from hers so I was a different kind of mother. I was a single working mother and she was a stay at home married mother. I had to worry about making a living, building a career, paying the bills, having relationships with men, and dealing with everything alone. My Mom had a happy marriage and a partner who gave her love and security, both financially and emotionally. As a single working mother; I never felt secure in any way and I was often stressed out, tired, financially broke, and lonely and I'm sure those things affected the way I dealt with my son. I didn't give Mom much trouble as I was growing up and she always had my Dad to back her up when she disciplined me but I had a difficult time with my son and I found his teenage years particularly hard to deal with alone.

To me "Velvet ropes" means that I am bound to my Mom forever and, although there have been times when that felt restrictive, I have always known that love is what binds us to each other.

Lynda
Retired social services executive, artist, author, mother, work in progress

Section VI

Intense love and deep connection....

Diane

Elizabeth

In the sheltered simplicity of the first days after a baby is born, one sees again the magical closed circle. The miraculous sense of two people existing only for each other.

~Anne Morrow Lindbergh

Where do I begin to talk about my mother? For starters, just her title, "Mom", elicits in me an overwhelming feeling of unconditional love. A love that I know is equally returned. From my earliest childhood memories, Mom was a constant. There wasn't a time she wasn't *there* in every sense of the word.

Our family was fortunate in that all of Dad's hard work, between his full time job, overtime and side work enabled Mom to stay home with me and my three sisters. It was Mom who bathed and dressed us as toddlers, made our lunches and got us out of the house in a timely manner in our school years and was there with open arms when we returned home. She helped us with homework, always prepared delicious homemade meals, read bedtime stories, and tucked us in at night. As we grew older, Mom taught us how to braid our hair, safely shave our legs and armpits, and apply just a hint of make-up that would not make us look any older than our age. She preferred us to sport the "natural" look but when we heard that expression we would dash for our best lipstick! Mom eased us through the horrors of getting zits on the end of our noses and the embarrassment of "bad-hair days". She gave us those secret womanly talks about the menstrual cycle and the birds and the bees and soothed our hearts at our first puppy love break-ups. She did all of this and more with such grace. Boy, what my poor father had to endure with five women in the house! Navigating the maze of stockings and bras hanging in the bathroom, hairdryers, curling irons, nail polish, make-up and PMS. (Ah, but that is another story!)

With four daughters of varying personalities, I must honestly say we were all treated equally. No one was favored or escaped punishment when warranted. Naturally, when boys entered the scene, us sisters didn't understand or agree with some of the restrictions that were placed on us for our protection. Looking back now, I am sorry for the times I ignored curfew and didn't agree that "Mom knows best" because I caused such worry and anxiety for my mother. In my mind, she had raised me properly. I knew right from wrong and wasn't going to do anything stupid or "wind up dead in a ditch somewhere" but Mom knew what dangers lingered outside the safety of our home and it gave her every right to be concerned. In maturity and my own parenthood today, I have come to understand and mimic those protective instincts. Pure love for the family unit was the reason behind all of Mom's words, rules and actions.

Speaking of love, I have always admired the relationship my parents have and I am so happy that they both recognized the magnificently wonderful mate they each chose. They complement each other well and trust and respect have always been given. When my Mom first met my Dad, her heart melted and she knew right away that there was no one else in the world for her. Needless to say, my goal as a teenager was to imitate my mother and find the right man to call my husband and then build a strong, close-knit family as she had. When marriage came for me, I thought I had done just that but years later some things changed and my fairytale didn't make it to the "happily-ever-after" part. The life of a single parent is one I never expected to have to pilot and I know that some of my decisions as such have not always met with my mother's approval. Thankfully, she has never had to walk in these shoes. It is a different and difficult path when you're alone and the decisions you make are completely your own burden to shoulder. I have always tried to make the best choices possible and I fully admit I have failed miserably at some. It is funny that no matter how old I get, my mother's seal of approval is always sought in all that I do. To this day, like a child, I never want to disappoint her and I believe that feeling will be in place until the day I depart this Earth. Sometimes I have felt that as a cross to bear but I have come to realize it must come from a feeling of admiration. To care so much about approval, support, and acceptance from someone must stem from admiring them and wanting to do things the right way as you know they would, confidently and without thinking about it twice. I don't think my Mom has ever regretted any of her important decisions because I believe she has always made them from the heart. There is something to be learned from that.

Thinking about child/parent relationships, I believe that those between mothers and daughters have a slight edge over all others. They are unique, special, and intimate and are ones that should be ultimately treasured. Women are complex creatures in that the depth of our emotional being can only be understood by another woman and what better a woman than the one that carried us in her womb, brought us into this world, and knows us so well? Whether it is good news, bad news, a simple or complex question that needs an answer or advice that is sought, it seems Mom is always the one called on first. Somehow she always has a way of making big problems seem smaller, dark times a little brighter and happy times happier.

Well, my sisters and I all made it through the learning years and admittedly didn't always make it easy for her but I believe we are all better women today due to the guidance, support, understanding, and love of our mother. We are all mothers ourselves now and we can be stronger ones because of the example that our mother has always set for us. We are all, including my mother, so close today. We have an unbreakable bond of friendship, respect, and admiration.

I wouldn't trade my mother for any other in the whole world. She wasn't an executive career woman, a world traveler, a famous actress or a distinguished author but she was and still is our family's CEO of love and what more can one ask than that?

Diane
Administrative assistant, mother

Where do I even begin to elaborate on my relationship with my mother? Just the mention of that beautiful word, and the memories that it invokes of the beautiful woman who carried me within her womb and raised me to be the woman I am today, brings me to tears...a salty mixture of sadness and of joy.

My Mom, Elizabeth Ann, was born on January 15, 1905, in Philadelphia, Pennsylvania. Her parents were Italian immigrants who had migrated to the United States, from Naples, in search of the American Dream. Life was not easy, but they never regretted the journey and always made sure that their children, who were born in the United States, knew that they were American, even while proudly holding true to their Italian heritage and customs. They raised their family in a predominately Italian neighborhood where my mother would live until she married my father in 1925, at the age of 20.

My mother was what you would have to describe as a mighty giant contained in a tiny body. Mom only stood about four feet and ten inches tall, but within that small space beat a heart as large as the world that she loved and served so well. She was truly one of the most unselfish and caring women that I have ever known...a woman who lived her entire life as an example of one word.....LOVE! She loved her family, her friends, her neighbors, the people that she passed on the street and, above all, she loved her God. You will never find her name written in any history book or listed in any "Who's Who", but the world around her was definitely enriched by her presence.

Mom was the second child, and oldest daughter, in a long line of offspring which totaled thirteen in all. Three babies died either at birth or shortly after, but the remaining ten (five girls and five boys) would live long into adulthood. Because of her birth rank, my mother did not have the luxury of living a carefree childhood. It fell upon her to help in the rearing of her younger brothers and sisters. She was pulled out of structured schooling after completing only fourth grade, and learned the rest of life's lessons while living them.

Days were filled with hard work. In those times, the woman's place was in the home and my mother never ventured much farther than the Italian market, which was within walking distance. Throughout her life, Mom never got behind the wheel of a car. All of her travels were on foot or by trolley cars until she met my father who was fortunate enough to own his own automobile. For the rest of her life, one of her greatest pleasures was to have my father take her on long rides through the neighboring countryside.

My mother and father did not follow the example set by Mom's parents...they only had three children. I was the youngest and was born when my sister was 16 and my brother was 10. I was to discover, much later in life, that my birth was definitely not planned. Our country was at war, money was scarce, and Mom and Dad already had a "rich man's family". A third child was the farthest thing from their minds. From the time that I was born, though, I knew that I was loved with all of the passion that a parent could have for a child. In a way, the difference in our ages made each of us feel like an only child. There was never any sibling rivalry because we each had quality time alone with our parents. There was never any favoritism shown. We all had our equal place in the framework of the family. Jealousy was never an issue. Through example, we learned only love...a love that has weathered every storm and is still as strong today as ever.

My parents truly had a marriage where certain lines were firmly drawn. Dad "brought home the bacon" and was so tired when he came home at night that he went to bed quite early. Mom raised the kids and took care of the home. Most of the parenting we received was from my mother. This was not to say that Dad didn't love his children, because he did. We, along with our mother, were his life. But it was Mom who fed us, made sure that all of our daily needs were met and, above all, showered us with love. Even the most mundane tasks were done with love, from brushing my curls in the morning while telling me a story (sometimes a well-known fairy tale and sometimes a tale from her own imagination), to tucking me into bed and listening to my prayers at night. The last conscious feeling that I had each evening was of my mother's lips kissing me good-night. I went to sleep knowing that I was safe and loved.

Being brought up in a home where there wasn't much quality time spent with both parents made me know that, when the time came, I would look for, and hopefully find, a man who would be able and willing to spend as much time with our children as I would. As much as I knew that my parents loved us and each other, I wanted more togetherness in my own marriage. My dream was for a husband that would be a father in actions as well as in name. I am thrilled to say that I, and my children, "hit the jackpot" in that department.

Mom's career was her family; although, once I was old enough to be left alone or with a sibling, she did get a little part-time job as a waitress in a neighborhood tea room. This wasn't really work for her because she loved being around people and it was second nature to prepare and serve food for them. After all, she had done that for most of her life for her sisters and brothers and for her own family. Most of the patrons would soon become her friends and would seek out my mother for her advice, comfort, or just for her willingness to listen. Everyone loved being around my mother. She had a bubbly personality, was always smiling, and her hands and feet were never idle. I used to think that she fit 36 hours into a 24 hour day.

Being the "baby" of the family definitely had its advantage. Long after my sister and brother had married and gone off to raise their own families, my mother and I were inseparable. We were together as much as we could reasonably be. I have wonderful memories of curling up on the couch at night, lying with my head on Mom's lap, watching a movie together... sometimes my head would bounce when her stomach shook with laughter and sometimes my tears over a sad ending would dampen her skirt. We always seemed to know what the other was thinking or feeling. It was as though we were one mind and one spirit, but in two bodies. I have never felt as close to another human being as I did with my Mommy.

Of course, we did have our differences. We were of two different generations and times were changing, but my morals were set in stone. Mom had seen to that. She had taught me right from wrong and my greatest fear was facing her wrath and disappointment if I should stray from the right path. I always said that I did the right things because it would have killed my mother if I hadn't. Not literally, of course, but I never wanted to hurt her in any way.

Mom showed me that you have to earn the title "Mom". It is easy to become a mother. All that takes is having one strong sperm meet up with the right egg and pushing a baby out after nine long months. But it's what you do with that helpless little infant after the cord is cut that makes the difference. It's a tough job and you have to be willing to put someone else's needs before your own. The pain of childbirth is nothing when compared to the trials and tribulations of rearing that child and the responsibility of sending that child out into the world someday, strong enough and with the right convictions, to make a difference in society. When each of my four daughters was born, I realized what an awesome responsibility had been handed to me. All of the lessons that my own mother had taught me through her actions came into play. I had a great role model to follow and I would do everything in my power to live up to her example. Life is not without its problems, and I am far from perfect, but I still do the best that I can to make my mother proud of what she made me. I can only hope and pray that my children, in retrospect, always know that I did my best and that they feel about me as I do about my own precious Mom.

When I was young and whenever my mother did or said something that I thought was "old-fashioned", I used to say that I would never do or say that to my own children. Well, guess what? I hear my mother's voice in the advice that I pass along to my daughters and now know they are probably saying the same thing about my words. But they will soon learn, if they haven't already, that some things are timeless. We are truly our mother's children and our mothers will live and speak through us long after we are gone. Just look into the mirror each morning. Who is it looking back? Look really hard. I do and, more and more each day, I see my mother reflected in my image.

In 1977, Mom left this world at the age of 72. It was much too soon for her to go, but I guess her work here on earth was finished. She had doled out all of the love she had to give and God was calling her to greener pastures. There is not a day that goes by that she is not in my thoughts and that my heart does not ache with missing her. She was my best friend, my confidant and "my Mommy". I know, without a doubt, that she is waiting somewhere, just out of sight, until she can once again gather me into her arms and place those tender lips upon my brow in that sweet kiss that will last throughout eternity. Until then, Mommy, sleep well. I love you!

Elizabeth
Wife, mother, grandmother

Section VII

A Writing Exercise

All sorrows can be borne if we put them in a story or tell a story about them.

~Isak Dinesen

A Writing Exercise

Write the story of you and your mother (or the woman who raised you) – it really is an interesting, and sometimes therapeutic, exercise. Remember to think about your mother as an individual person, not just as the woman who raised you. Here are some questions I developed to help stimulate thoughts and memories:

1. Think about your mother's history before you were on the scene:
   a. What is/was her name and year she was born?
   b. Where was she born and where did she grow up?
   c. How many brothers/sisters did she have and where was she in the birth order?
   d. How old was she when she got married?
   e. Did she go to college or have a career before marriage?
   f. Did she work after marrying?

2. How would you describe your parent's marriage? How did it influence your love relationships?
3. If you have siblings, did you feel that your mother had a favorite? What kind of feelings did that evoke in you?
4. How would you describe your mother's personality?
5. What important lessons did you learn from your mother about what it means to be a woman? What type of a role model was she?
6. What important lessons did you learn from your mother about being a mother?
7. Did you ever consciously try to be different than her as a woman and/or as a mother? If so, in what ways?
8. How would you describe your adult relationship with your mother?
9. How important is your mother's approval of you and/or the choices you make?

10. In what way, if any, do you relate to the phrase “velvet ropes: ties that bind mothers and daughters”?

Whether negative or positive, good or bad, we have all been greatly influenced by our mothers (or the women who raised us) so be honest with yourself and tell the real story!

The Author and Her Mother, Brenda.

Lynda Linke *is a retired social services executive, artist and published author. She attended the School of Visual Arts in NYC and earned a BA from Thomas A. Edison College in New Jersey. Inspired by a long-time interest in family relationships, she collected the mother/daughter stories of 20 women (including her own) and added her original illustrations to create Velvet Ropes. Lynda resides in Florida with her dog, Stella.*

www.lyndalinke.com

CPSIA information can be obtained at www.ICGtesting.com
Printed in the USA
LVOW081857111112
306815LV00004B/7/P

9 781621 412151